Golem's Shadow
The Fall of Sherlock Holmes

Petr Macek

Paperback ISBN 9781780927268
ePub ISBN 978-1-78092-727-5
PDF ISBN 978-1-78092-728-2

Published in the UK by MX Publishing
335 Princess Park Manor, Royal Drive,
London, N11 3GX

www.mxpublishing.com
Cover design by www.staunch.com

CONTENTS

Foreword

Although many years have passed since Sherlock Holmes left public life, readers still ask me to remember the famous detective in a column, article or memoir. Hardly a week goes by in which I do not receive a letter from one celebrated publication or another asking me to set down our other adventures in literary form.

To be perfectly honest, I had no desire to do so. My friend's peace of mind was for more important to me than the barrage of figures and fat cheques promised to me for a few lines of print. On the other hand, I marvelled at the joy with which Holmes reacted to these requests.

"Give the vultures what they want," he would say with a sharp laugh, casting the publishers' letters into the fireplace, which is where they belonged.

Holmes had a weakness for the tabloids. He said that one always found something interesting in them. He was never much interested in politics or international affairs; he was much happier reading about crime and murder. It was only on the rarest of occasions that he consented to investigate a political affair and that only through the intercession of the highest government office or at the beckoning of his elder brother Mycroft.

Similar thoughts when through my mind as I read another letter from my former publisher, Mr Doyle. He again asked me to reconsider my objections and urged me to accept the handsome fee that he proffered. After much hesitation, I therefore finally decided to return to my memories of those grand days that I had spent alongside the great detective. Not for profit, mind you, but for the warm feeling that I experience while setting down our cases. In recent years, moreover, my contact with Holmes had been restricted to correspondence and occasional visits to his farm. To once again spend time with

Sherlock Holmes, even if only on paper, was so appealing that I finally succumbed.

I am going through my notes from that time to see if I can find a case gripping enough to captivate today's readers. To my surprise, at the bottom of an old trunk I found notes from a case that I have barely thought about in years, despite its tragic nature.

The case is shrouded in such horror that I had to suppress it deep in my subconscious. Now I again summon it to the light of day, where I hope it will lose some of its morbid fascination, knowing full well what inevitably must follow.

John H. Watson, M.D.

April 23, 1924

I

The Jilted Bride

It was a cold and damp early autumn day, some three years after the death of our dear Queen Victoria, and almost ten years after my friend's return from his great chase after Moriarty. By five in the evening the shadows on the streets were already starting to grow longer and an hour later the new electric lamps shone like small islands of light in a sea of darkness. In the windows of the apartment in Baker Street the first drops of rain appeared.

Sherlock Holmes had been beset by gloom and depression ever since the news of the death of Irene Adler. For weeks now he had wallowed in a kind of stupor of ennui. There was no case on the horizon, and not even the specialist essays or the chemistry experiments that usually filled these barren times succeeded in diverting him.

Despite my beseeching he took refuge in his old vices.

Cocaine once again had him in thrall. My wife and I had to travel outside London, and upon returning I found Holmes unshaven and delirious. His brilliant mind could not stand being idle and succumbed to the drug.

I immediately removed all of his equipment and resolved to fight for his soul.

It took me several weeks but in the end I succeeded in bringing Holmes back to reality. Naturally there were violent mood swings and paroxysms when I cut off the supply of the opiate. He would go into a panic and not know the world around him. But these seemed to be getting weaker and then they apparently subsided.

I again moved in with Holmes and constantly tried to keep him occupied. I ordered our landlady Mrs Hudson to wake us as late as possible and I took him on long walks, which helped lessen his irritability.

One afternoon we were walking about the city where I was trying to distract Holmes with the sight of several new modern-style buildings rising up not far from our lodgings. For a moment he became indignant about their monstrousness, but a moment later he again pushed his cap down over his forehead and with his gaze fixed on the ground marched with his characteristic swaying gait back to the house.

"Come, Watson," he mumbled irritably. "It is time for the evening edition. God willing we will find something interesting in it!"

I turned around and gave up the day's attempt to rid him of his melancholy.

We returned home and soon dusk turned into evening. Our good landlady, who was also sorely affected by my friend's condition, tried to lift his spirits in her own special way, by serving us the most delectable meals. The repast concluded with an excellent dessert: a chocolate cake with homemade raspberry jam. This could not leave Holmes cold, and as we sat in armchairs drinking coffee in front of the fireplace he even managed a faint smile.

"Still it's distressing, don't you think?" he said as we listened to the logs crackling in the fire.

"What do you mean?"

"Every second somewhere in the world a crime is afoot, and cruel fate does not so much as send me an ordinary pickpocket," he sighed.

I thought to placate him with a white lie. It even occurred to me to go to Inspector Lestrade's office tomorrow to see if he knew of a crime with which to divert Holmes.

But suddenly there was an insistent knocking at the door! Holmes's aquiline profile straightened.

Mrs Hudson hurried downstairs to open the door and the detective listened carefully. We could hear the pattering of quick footsteps rushing up the stairs to our lodgings. At that late hour it could be only a client in trouble!

Holmes jumped up to open the door. Before us stood a young woman dressed in white, her hand frozen in the air in a knocking motion.

The hem of her wedding dress was muddy and the rain had turned her blonde coiffure into a limp and tangled mess. A shawl was thrown over her shoulders and there was a beautiful diamond brooch fastened on her breast. Despite the inclement weather she had a charming air, which captivated me as well as the detective, who was usually immune to female charms.

"Mr Sherlock Holmes?" she asked breathlessly.

"Do I have the honour of addressing Miss Annabelle Watts?" said Holmes bowing gallantly."Or is it already Lady St. John-Smythe?"

"How did you recognise me?" asked the bride gasping for breath and accepting our invitation to enter the living room. "Have we met before?"

"Never," he said. "Your unusual attire reveals how you probably spent the day. I read your family's notice in today's *Times*. The Church of St. George was prepared for a number of days for the wedding of the daughter of the wealthiest London coal magnate and the young Lord James St. John-Smythe!"

"But there must be dozens of weddings in London every day!"

"Not ones where the bride has a dress from the best dressmaker in all of England. And judging by the condition of said dress I gather that you got very wet on the way. It started to rain here just a moment ago, and according to the direction of the drops on the window I presume that the wind is blowing the rain from the east, where the Church of St. George is located. But perhaps I am mistaken."

"You are absolutely correct!"

The woman looked at him with astonishment and took a seat at the fireplace. Holmes poured her a glass of brandy. Despite the brandy and the warm fireplace she was trembling all over.

"May I bring you a shawl?" I offered.

She shook her head. She removed her wet and muddy shoes, and stretched her feet towards the fire. As a doctor I could not fail to notice the anatomical perfection of her calf.

"Tell me why the wedding did not take place," said Holmes.

"How did you know that?" she cried.

Holmes sighed.

"Why would an apparently spurned bride seek me out at the beginning of her wedding night? And leaving all deduction aside, the problem is very clearly attested by the absence of a wedding band on your finger."

Miss Watts stared at the ring finger of her left hand.

"Indeed the wedding did not take place," she confirmed, and her eyes welled with tears. "I left the church in a daze and wandered the streets aimlessly until it started to rain. Don't be angry that I bothered you! You must help me!"

"I will do what I can. But you must tell me exactly what happened."

"James never appeared," she said, her lips quivering.

"I'm afraid these things happen, my dear," I said. "The young man simply lost his nerve. He no doubt loves you passionately and is now sitting at home with his conscience gnawing at him. In a couple of days he will show up at your doorstep to beg your forgiveness. It is embarrassing and unpleasant, but it is not something that we can influence."

"It is not so," she cried, looking beseechingly at Holmes. "My father immediately drove to his London flat in order to fetch him. But he did not find him anywhere!"

"Could he be hiding out at a friend's?" asked the detective.

"Perhaps," she sobbed. "Except that even stranger things have happened! My father then went to the Clariton Hotel, where James's parents are staying. They came from the countryside for the wedding. But he discovered that Sir St. John-

6

Smythe Sr. and Lady St. John-Smythe had left in the morning immediately after breakfast!"

"Presumably they intended to return home right after the ceremony," I said.

"Except that they never came to the ceremony! My father is furious and I fear what he will do when he finds James. He thinks that I am the victim of a fraud! It seems that James borrowed a lot of money from him before the wedding."

"And what would you like us to do?" asked Holmes, leaning back in his armchair and lighting his pipe from the embers of the fireplace. He let out a fragrant cloud of smoke and threw the ember back into the fire.

"Do you want us to find him first?"

She nodded.

"It is not the type of investigation that I usually engage in."

"Please find him! Otherwise papa will kill him!"

"Why?"I asked. "If everything you have told us is true then–"

"I don't believe what my father says," she said passionately. "I know that James is incapable of these things! Will you help me, gentlemen? Surely something terrible has happened to him!"

Holmes and I exchanged glances. On the surface, at least, the story was as bright as day. Annabelle's father seemed to understand the situation correctly. On the other hand, it could occupy Holmes for some little while and help cure his depression and eradicate the memory of his vice.

The detective threw his head back and exhaled another cloud of smoke. Only those who knew him as well as I did could tell how quickly his brain was working. He was already considering and arranging the facts of the case, which often appeared logical only to him.

"Very well," he said after a long pause. "I will track down your fiancé."

"Oh, Mr Holmes, thank you!"Miss Watts cried. "If you find him I will be so grateful! Of course I will pay all your expenses and fees, I have money saved up. And if that is not enough, I can give you a deposit."

She removed her diamond brooch and placed it on the table.

Holmes picked it up carefully and looked at it with amusement.

"My child, we will discuss payment only if I succeed."

He held the brooch up to the light of the fireplace.

"A beautiful piece. A family heirloom, am I right?"

"Yes," she replied. "Years ago my father gave it to my late mother as an engagement present."

The detective examined the remarkable brooch for a moment longer and then returned it.

"You would be vastly overpaying me. It no doubt means a lot to you."

He stood up.

"Watson, please ask Mrs Hudson to call a coach."

I quickly ran downstairs to fulfil his request. When I returned our visitor was standing at the door ready to depart.

"One more small matter," said Holmes. "I assume that you have a photograph of your fiancé with you. Could you leave it with me?"

"Of course; I had completely forgotten!"

She took from her purse a rectangular likeness.

"This is an official photograph taken on the occasion of our engagement!"

In the photograph Miss Watts was sitting in an armchair and standing next to her holding her arm was a handsome young man. He had short, brushed back hair with large trimmed sideburns, a short moustache and a pointed beard. The couple looked happy.

"Thank you, that is all I need for now," said Holmes, examining the photograph carefully. "I shall try to have some answers in a few days."

Miss Watts nodded and ran downstairs, Miss Hudson closing the door behind her. We watched her from the window. She tucked her head under her scarf and quickly ran across the street under torrents of rain and disappeared into the waiting coach. The coachman jerked the reins and the coach trundled into the darkness.

"We have a case," I said turning to Holmes happily and closing the curtains.

"Yes," he said thoughtfully. "It will no doubt be interesting."

It was no longer the aggrieved lament of that morning. It was again my good old friend. I could not help but smile; at least until Holmes placed his violin under his chin and began to play in order to help him think.

The prospect of a peaceful night's sleep was lost.

II

Bookseller in Trouble

The next morning it was my turn to wake up feeling irritable. A long sleepless night, the result of the high "c" produced by Holmes's violin, was to blame. I arose in my cold bedroom in a foul mood, stuck my bare feet into my slippers, and dressed only in a housecoat headed for breakfast.

Our drawing room was a study in contrast to my bedroom. It was as though Holmes's mood and the London weather were in some way aligned. Autumn sunshine flooded through the open windows. The sky had cleared as though by the wave of a magician's wand. The wood in the fire was again burning dutifully, and the warm air was pervaded by the delicious aroma of coffee.

Holmes was already sitting fully dressed at breakfast, surrounded by the early editions of *The Times* and *The Morning Chronicle,* and evidently eating with relish. There was no sign of the symptoms that had plagued him for the last week.

"Good morning, Watson!" he said cheerfully.

"At least *you* slept well," I grumbled and sat across from him.

Holmes wiped his mouth with a napkin, set aside the newspapers and poured me a cup of coffee.

"What's the matter, Watson? Has an autumn melancholy befallen you? Look how beautiful the morning is! A joy to behold!"

I cursed his cheerfulness with a cold glance and resolved not to keep my grievances to myself time.

"Holmes, I am glad that you are in such good spirits, which is why I hesitate to remind you of your behaviour these past few days!"

"*Tempora mutantur, nos et mutamur in illis*,*" he said laughing loudly and handed me the coffee. "Forgive my petulance!"

I placed the cup on the table and began eating the delectable eggs and bacon which Mrs Hudson had prepared.

"I do not reproach you for it, but for God's sake, why must you play so long into the night?"

"I am so selfish," he said ruefully. "It did not occur to me that my music might disturb you! Is that why you are so irritable?"

"It was not the music. But what was that howling sound?"

"Oh! Do you mean this?"he asked, humming a piece of the hateful melody. "I recently found in a bookshop the notes to a certain chamber piece by an unknown composer. So I was practising it a little."

"The composer is lucky that he is unknown," I said. "What is it?"

"It is called *Möhrentanz*!" said Holmes, tactfully skipping over my comment. "Unfortunately, our dear ancestors were not yet sufficiently knowledgeable of keys."

"It is in my view no excuse!"

"Relax and eat your breakfast!"he said waving his hand. "We have work to do!"

And he returned to his papers. It seemed that the laxity of the past weeks was buried and forgotten.

"The case from yesterday evening?"

"Do you know of another?"he said, looking at me quizzically over *The Times*. "According to today's report London is the most peaceful city on Earth! Were it not for Monsieur Loubet and the entente**they would have nothing to write about!"

I ate hurriedly while Holmes finished reading. When the landlady came to clear the table, we were both ready to depart.

We stepped out into the street and slowly headed in the direction of the nearest coach stand.

It looked as though the day would indeed be fine. The streets had dried after the night's rain and brooks gurgled somewhere down in the underground canals. The air smelled of fresh bread and the streets echoed with the cries of stallholders.

In a pleasant frame of mind we came to the main street and walked to the coach stand at the curb. We chose an open coach pulled by two well-fed brown horses. I sat down comfortably in the direction of travel, but just then Holmes with his foot on the running board heard the call of a street paperboy.

"Scandal in millionaire family! Daughter of mine owner deceived by confidence man!"cried a ten-year-old boy at the top of his lungs.

Holmes went up to him and pushed a few coins into his hand. The boy gave him a newspaper and doffed his grubby hat.

"Our client will not be pleased," I said uneasily.

"Least of all her father," the detective added as he scanned the headlines of the latest edition of *The Post*. "This paper is not known for its discretion. But there is nothing new for us here."

"Where are we going now?"

Holmes cast aside the paper and sat down next to me.

"Tothill Street!" he shouted to the coachman. "Club No.1!"

The coachman spat a wad of tobacco on the pavement and smacked his horses. They set off sluggishly and for a while we moved through the busy city traffic.

"Miss Watts told me yesterday evening when you went to fetch Mrs Hudson that her fiancé is a member of this luxurious gentlemen's club," said Holmes. "As it only accepts new members at the recommendation of two existing members, perhaps we can find someone who will give us some more information about our young Lord St. John-Smythe."

"Does it not strike you as odd that she herself knows so little about him?"

"For a girl in love the voice of the heart is usually enough," he said, shaking his head.

The rest of the way he proceeded to discourse on the consequences of such foolish and hasty acquaintance.

The coach pulled up in front of an opulent house to which stairs lined with metal wrought iron railings led to the entrance. The first floor consisted of a red brick facade; the upper floors of light orange plaster. The entrance was equipped with a heavy oak door knocker, located between elegant columns and under decorated arcades. The windows behind the trimmed shrubs had their curtains closed, so we could not see inside.

I went straight to the door but Holmes held me back.

"It will be better, Watson, if we do not reveal our real names," he said to me and then mumbled a few instructions.

I gently knocked on the door. A moment later it opened and a curious doorman peered through the crack.

"What do you want, gentlemen?"

"I am Professor Wat... chester and this is Mr Dawson," I said. "A certain friend of mine is a member of the club. I need to speak with him."

"What is his name?"

"Sir James St. John-Smythe," I said as nonchalantly as possible.

The doorman opened the door a little more. He was old and wizened and wore a red cap, a coat with shiny buttons and a carefully starched collar.

"The young gentleman is not here today," he said. "He has not been here in almost a week. But after all yesterday he got married, you know."

"Has he?" I said, trying to sound surprised. "I just returned yesterday from a long business trip in America. Wouldn't you know it!"

"Indeed," said the doorman nodding. "And to a very good family! Do you know the coal merchant, Watts? The bride is his daughter!"

"Really?" I exclaimed, taking advantage of the fact that he had apparently not read the morning paper.

"Yes. By now he is probably with the young lady on their honeymoon!"

"That is annoying! I so do need to talk to him. Do you know when he will be back?"

"I'm afraid not," he said shrugging his shoulders. "But perhaps Mr Robins will know something. He is one of his sponsors. Would you like to speak with him?"

"That would be most kind of you," I said, nodding gratefully and doffing my hat.

Holmes and I walked into the vestibule and followed the doorman through a hallway decorated with pictures to a drawing room reserved for visitors.

"Please wait here; I will return directly."

We hung our coats and sat down in lounge chairs. I looked around the room, which was hazy with cigar smoke. Men sat in armchairs and spoke together in hushed tones.

While we waited for the doorman to return, Holmes leaned over to me.

"Must you lay it on so thick, Watson?"he whispered.

I wanted to protest, but the doorman re-entered with a young gentleman in a cream suit and a white cravat. He looked elegant and confident. His short hair was brushed back with brilliantine and his smooth white face shone with innocence.

"Good day, my name is Mark Robins," he said. "With whom do I have the pleasure?"

We introduced ourselves, naturally using our assumed named, and the young nobleman sat down with us eagerly.

"What can I do for you, Professor?" he asked.

I repeated the story about my return from America and waited to see if he would take the bait. But when I asked whether he knew when St. John-Smythe would return, he just laughed.

"Forgive me," he said, when he saw my baffled expression. "I have no idea. If I were him I would not show my face in London for a good while yet. I was at the wedding yesterday and imagine that rogue did not show up! The father of the bride is furious and has sworn to kill him!"

Holmes frowned.

"Has he always been so reckless?"Robins asked.

"I don't remember," I said evasively to avoid possible disclosure.

"And how long have you known him, Mr Robins?" asked Holmes.

"About a year. We are not best friends, but we see each other regularly. He comes from somewhere in Surrey, but these country aristocrats are all so secretive."

"You sponsored him for membership in the club?"

"Oh yes. A mutual friend of ours asked me to do it. Two votes are required for membership and James did not know anyone else in the club besides us."

"May I ask who the second sponsor is?"

"Of course. Mr Phillip Gottfried, who owns the bookshop on Victoria Street, not far from here. Perhaps he will know more."

"We shall not detain you longer," said the detective rising. "Shall we go, Professor?"

We wished Mr Robins good-day and left the club.

"That was not very helpful, was it?" I said when we were back outside in the noisy street.

"On the contrary!" said Holmes, evidently surprised at my stupidity.

"What of use did you discover?"I asked, wondering what I had missed.

"Let me first sort out the facts and draw appropriate conclusions. But it is definitely getting more interesting!"

He whistled for a coach. We jumped in and for the whole trip he remained doggedly silent.

The wheels clattered on the pavement and soon we found ourselves in front of a ground floor shop with a large window and signboard saying *Gottfried & Co*. It was the bookshop where Holmes hoped to find the second friend from Club No. 1.

We passed beneath the swinging sign and entered the cosy shop. A clerk was packing books. A bell over the door alerted him to our presence.

"We would like to speak with Mr Gottfried about a private matter," I said to the clerk."Could you call him?"

A moment later a tall man appeared. He had blazing red hair and wore round glasses on his elongated and sullen face.

"How may I help you, gentlemen?" he asked curiously.

"I am a friend of Lord St. John-Smythe and..."

I did not manage to say more, for the man grabbed me by the lapels and shook me roughly.

"Where is that rogue!" he shouted.

"I don't understand," I cried. "What are you talking about?"

Had not Holmes intervened I think he would have struck me.

"Violence serves no purpose," he remarked coolly and removed the bookseller's hand from my neck. "I will tell you the truth. I am private detective Sherlock Holmes and this is my associate Dr Watson."

The bookseller let go of me and looked at us with surprise.

"Why the charade?"

"We are in the service of a certain lady who desires to find Lord St John-Smythe. We hoped that you could tell us your friend's present whereabouts."

The man flushed red with anger.

"Friend? Not anymore! That scoundrel stole several thousand pounds from me!"

"Did you report it to the police?"

"No, not yet. At first I assumed it was a misunderstanding and that we would sort it all out at his wedding. But after yesterday's events and after what I read in today's papers I have no other alternative!"

"How long have you known him?"

"About half a year. We met at a party after the premiere of a play and since then we have seen each other occasionally. He travelled to London always at least once a month."

"But in Club No.1 you are considered close friends; you are his sponsor!"

The bookseller frowned and motioned to the clerk to leave.

"He asked me to sponsor him because he didn't have anyone else. I had the highest regard for him; he never gave me reason to suspect his motives. That is why I even asked another member of the club to sponsor him too."

"And so he ingratiated himself into your favour in order to take advantage of you," I said.

"I admit that I was duped. In fact, a few weeks later we saw each other even less than usual. He often travelled to the continent, supposedly on business."

Holmes looked around the cosy shop, walking among the shelves with their old volumes.

"How did he steal the money?"

The man grew even more sombre.

"I am partly to blame," he admitted. "I thought that he was an able businessman, and when I opened this shop, basically as a hobby, I asked for his advice. He offered to help me with the accounts and I was happy to accept, as I have no knowledge of bookkeeping. He said it was a favour for my having sponsored his membership in the club."

"A true favour indeed!"

"A few days ago I discovered that the account was empty!" said the bookseller clenching his fists. "Suppliers have started knocking on my door and I do not have the money to pay my debts. If I do not find him my business will be ruined!"

"We will let you know if our investigation succeeds," said the detective.

"I will be grateful to you, sirs," he said. "And I believe that you will succeed. I am a great admirer of yours; I have read about all of your cases!"

"My chronicler exaggerates," said Holmes, casting a glance at me, but I knew that he was pleased. He would never admit it, but he enjoyed his fame.

"I will wait then before notifying the police!"

"That would be most helpful," said the detective. "Nothing disrupts detective work more than the involvement of amateurs."

He put on his cap and with a bow and a promise to keep him informed about the progress of our investigation left the shop, leaving the bookseller to his cares.

I joined him outside on the pavement.

"Did that help us?"

"But of course, Watson!" he said. "Do you still not understand what is going on?"

I had to allow that I did not.

"Everyone says the same thing; they don't know where he is!"

"They told us everything that I need to know for the time being."

"Then I must not be listening to the same conversation!"

"I can see that, my dear friend," said Holmes. "Go home and tell Mrs Hudson to wait for me with lunch. I have one more important matter to attend to."

And without further delay he turned on his heels and headed in the direction of Westminster Abbey.

I knew from past experience that it was futile to try to extract more information from him, so I took a coach back to Baker Street.

*   Lat. – Times change, and we change with them.
** The Entente Cordiale was a series of agreements between the United Kingdom and France, marking the start of the alliance against Germany and Austria-Hungary that fought the First World War.

III

The Man Who Knew Oscar Wilde

Holmes failed to return at the appointed time. Like so many times before he was apparently delaying an explanation of why he had so suddenly left me standing alone on Victoria Street. Since he did not even appear that afternoon, I had to find something else to do. My wife*was at that time spending several weeks at her relatives. And I was sharing my medical practice with a young practitioner, to whom in truth I was transferring my work more and more often.

I did not want to wait at home worrying about Holmes and waste perhaps one of the last fine days of the year. I dressed and went for a stroll in Regent's Park, whose natural scenery is so pleasant and tranquil. By chance I met a few friends, a married couple who was friends with my late wife Mary**. We talked for a long time, so that I hardly noticed it was getting darker and that the streetlamps were coming on.

I took a coach home so that I would not have to trudge alone through the dark streets. As I paid the coachman my eyes strayed to our windows in the expectation of seeing backlit curtains and perhaps Holmes's silhouette. But to my surprise the windows were dark.

"Good evening, Doctor."

The voice startled me. It came from the neighbouring entranceway, but I immediately recognised the face of the local policeman who often patrolled our street at night.

He stopped by the streetlamp and leaned against it. He seemed to want some diversion from the tedium of his rounds, so I chatted with him for a while. Moths flitted around the dirty glass lamps above our heads, casting eerie shadows on the wall opposite the building.

"Dark at your place. Is Mr Holmes out on another case?"

I replied that I had no idea.

Indeed I had thought that Holmes would already be home and I felt a strange sense of anxiety.

"If he's found a clue somewhere then he has forgotten the time entirely, you know him!" said the policeman.

Suddenly a cold wind gusted into the street. I stuck my hands deeper into my pockets. The policeman interpreted my gesture as a sign that the conversation was over. He lightly touched his helmet in a casual salute and continued on his way. A moment later he vanished into the darkness.

As I headed upstairs to our lodgings I first stopped in to see Mrs Hudson. I wanted to inform her that I was home and to inquire about Holmes.

"But Mr Holmes returned as soon as you left!" she said with surprise.

I was taken aback because it had certainly been dark in the window. Holmes was not in the habit of spending the evening in the dark. I remembered how a hired killer had once snuck into our lodgings, and I imagined the worst. With Mrs Hudson at my heels I ran upstairs and threw open the door of the apartment.

My eyes fell on a figure slumped in a chair by the fireplace. The detective raised his head and looked at us with surprise.

"To what do I owe such the dramatic entrance?"

"Holmes, you frightened me!"I cried. "Why are you sitting in the dark?"

"I think better this way," he said.

"In the dark?"

"Yes, there are no distractions. You must not be so anxious, Watson."

Mrs Hudson laughed and asked whether we wanted supper. After a late lunch and the nervous tension I had no thought of food, and Holmes usually did not eat supper at all. I declined for both of us, but my friend had another surprise in store for me.

"If you still have a piece of that excellent pie I would be delighted!"

Mrs Hudson went to fetch the pie, which was made with a truly excellent marmalade, and I dropped wearily into an armchair next to Holmes. It was all too much for me.

"Where have you been wandering all day?"

"I was at the registry office," he replied. "I got held up there longer than I expected, but in the end I found what I was looking for. And then I still had to send a telegram. I expect that the answer should be coming shortly!"

"Excuse me?" I said uncomprehendingly.

The detective tapped his index finger on his ear. I too listened, but except for the muffled cries of children playing on the pavement I heard nothing. But then there really was a deafening banging on the front door, followed by the angry scolding of our landlady. A few seconds later Billy, a freckled teenager whom we sometimes used as an errand boy, burst into the room.

At his heels was Mrs Hudson with the pie for Holmes.

"He almost crashed into me the way he ran!"she said angrily.

"It's my fault," said Holmes apologetically." I told him to hurry at all costs as soon as he got a reply."

He thanked Mrs Hudson for the pie and sent her away. When the door had closed behind her he looked at Billy and reached out to him with his bony hand in anticipation.

"Well?"

The boy took a folded telegram out of his pocket and looked hungrily at the pie. My friend noticed this, of course, and while reading gestured for him to take some. Billy's eyes lit up, he grabbed the pie and ran swiftly out the door as though he feared that Holmes might change his mind.

"Excellent!" said Holmes placing the missive on the table.

I read it too, but its meaning escaped me:

NOT FOR A FEW MONTHS NOW STOP
CONSTABLE HUTCHINSON

That was all. I was no wiser than I had been in the morning. My friend surely realised this and my befuddlement greatly amused him. He lounged in his armchair warming his hands over the fire.

"Tomorrow we will go on a short trip. Will you have time?"

He was apparently referring to my practice, which I had been neglecting of late.

"Of course," I said. "I promised Williams that I would be back on Monday, but he certainly won't mind if I ask him to work for a few more days. May I know where we are going, Holmes?"

"To the country," he said.

He seemed in no mood to tell me more.

"Can you at least tell me how you knew that Billy was coming even before he knocked on the door?"

Holmes looked at me with amusement.

"Watson, what do you see when you look out the window?" he asked.

"Nothing," I said, wondering what he was on about.

"Correct. There is nothing there. At this hour not even children are playing outside. When I heard their cries I knew that it could only be the circle of street urchins that always surrounds Billy. And indeed it was."

As always whenever he revealed his deductive reasoning to me it all seemed so elementary.

* * *

The next morning we set off on our journey. The weather was just as pleasant as it had been the day before, but occasionally a

23

cloud swept across the sky and plunged the city into shadow. Even more pleasing to me was that for the last two nights Holmes had had no thoughts of cocaine and the paroxysms that had recently afflicted him had ceased.

He was in an unusually talkative mood in the coach and I even learned the destination of our trip: the small town of Chiphead in West Surrey.

When we arrived at King's Cross station our train was already waiting on the third platform. A short while later the locomotive whistled and let out a cloud of hot steam and the train slowly began to pick up speed. Holmes was absorbed in a newspaper and I gazed out the window at the passing scenery.

We arrived at our destination around noon. We were the only passengers to disembark at the small station of the sleepy town. The station attendant, who was visibly disappointed that we did not have any suitcases and thus had no chance of a tip, asked us curiously where we were headed. Holmes ignored his question and asked whether there was a good inn in town.

"Just the Unicorn, sir. It's on the main street, you can't miss it."

We left the old station building and in a few minutes found the inn. Holmes announced that he wanted to eat and I agreed wholeheartedly. As a doctor I knew the importance of regular meals and I was happy that Holmes had regained his appetite.

The inn was cosy and clean, if somewhat provincial in appearance. We ordered fish and gazed at the hunting trophies on the walls while we waited.

"What are we doing here?"

Holmes raised his eyebrows.

"Working, naturally!"

"Can you tell me anything specific?"

"But it is elementary, my dear Watson! At the registry office yesterday I found records of James St. John-Smythe and his parents. The name is not invented, as I had at first suspected;

these people actually exist. They inhabit an estate about twenty minutes from here. Where else would we begin our investigation?"

I had no counterargument.

"What about the telegram?"

"I asked the commander of the local garrison if the inhabitants of the house had recently left Chiphead," he said. "You know the answer. It is clear that whoever pretended to be Lord St. John-Smythe in London and in the family of Miss Watts was a fraud. We cannot save our client's illusions about her fiancé, but perhaps we will find her father's and Mr Gottfried's money."

After a good lunch we hired a coach and instructed the driver to take us to the St. John-Smythe estate. We hoped that there we would find some answers.

Some three and a half miles from Chiphead our gaze fell upon an old Elizabethan house, surrounded on one side by forest and from the other by a wild plain above which circled a family of cawing rooks. At first glance the building looked grim. Its grey walls and blackened roof cast long shadows over the ground. Most of the windows were shuttered; probably only the main wing was inhabited.

We trundled up the driveway bordered with tall, naked trees, whose branches had long since outgrown their intended shape and intertwined in a kind of roof above our coach.

Leaves crunched beneath the wheels of the coach and flew about on every side in the breeze. When we got out of the coach the wet leaves stuck to our shoes. I did not like it here. The gloom of this place made me feel apprehensive and I had to reassure myself that our driver would indeed wait for us at the gate.

As always Holmes was immune to such moods and he knocked on the door with determination.

The door was opened by a sullen butler. Obviously they did not have many visitors.

"My name is Holmes and this is Dr Watson," said the detective.

"You are expected," said the butler, stepping aside and bowing slightly.

We entered a cold hall in the middle of which was a wide staircase covered with a dark red runner. Two large doors led from the hall, one on each side. The butler directed us into the room on the left and invited us to sit down on the sofa. We politely declined his offer of a drink and he went to fetch the master of the house.

"Holmes, how is it that we are expected?"I whispered when the servant had left.

"I haven't the foggiest," he admitted.

It wasn't often that I heard him say that.

We waited in the room alone for several minutes. On the walls there were large paintings depicting famous battles and over the sad fireplace there hung a portrait of a distinguished-looking grey-haired man.

"That is my late husband," said a high-pitched voice from the door, cutting like a dagger through the silence of the drawing room. "He died a few months ago."

We turned and saw a small woman with greying hair tightly pulled back in a bun. Her thin figure clothed in a plain dark dress with high collar appeared in the door like a statue.

"Have you come for my son?" she asked.

We nodded sheepishly.

"Follow me," she said.

We walked after her into a distant wing of the house. The corridors looked even worse than the drawing room. They were cold and dark, just like the whole house. There was no furniture, except for some rusted armour, a monument to the estate's bygone days.

She led us to a room in the right wing of the building, into which autumn sunshine streamed through the large windows. Unlike the rest of the house this room was surprisingly warm and hospitable.

Near the window a young man was sitting in a wheelchair with his back to us.

Upon hearing the door open he turned the chair to face us. I could immediately tell that he was paralysed from the waist down. His face was haggard and tired-looking.

"Mother?" he said, looking at the woman quizzically.

"This is Dr Watson," she said, pushing me forward. "I asked Professor Abbott to send us another specialist. I don't believe that—"

"It's been two years already!" he interrupted her, his voice filled with pain. "When will you finally accept it and stop spending what little we have left on pointless doctors? I did, you must as well!"

He turned the wheelchair towards me.

"What did my mother and the professor tell you? That I sometimes feel a tingling in my feet. It is nonsense; it is only what they hope!"

We immediately realised that some erroneous assumptions had been made.

"I am afraid there has been a misunderstanding," said Holmes."We have come to see the young gentleman, and my companion is indeed a doctor, but we have not spoken with Professor Abbott. We are here on another matter."

Lady St. John-Smythe looked at us as though we were aliens.

"Leave this house at once or I will have you removed!" she commanded.

Holmes nodded his head gravely, but did not take a step.

"I ask only one thing. Do you recognise the man in this photograph?"

He took Miss Watts's engagement photograph from his breast pocket and showed it to the woman.

She puckered her eyebrows and frowned. Clearly she recognised him.

"*Enfant terrible!*" she cried. "What has he done? He better not want money from us! Leave at once!"

"Who is it?" asked the young man in the wheelchair.

Holmes handed him the photograph.

"Henry?"

"Do you know him?"

"Yes, certainly!" said the woman angrily. "He spent several months in this house! He feigned friendship and took the liberty of allowing us to support him – the parasite!"

"Leave us alone, I will talk with these gentlemen in private!" the young man said to his mother.

"But–"

"Please!"

The lady clearly disproved but reluctantly left the room.

The young man waited until his mother was out of earshot and brought his wheelchair closer to us.

"Who are you?" he asked.

"Sherlock Holmes, private detective."

"I've read about you."

"Then you trust that I need to know the answers to my questions!"

"Why?"

"I need to find this man on account of some unpleasant business."

"Very well," said the young man, furrowing his brow. "I met Henry about two years ago at a rather boisterous party. He was amusing and agreeable, and we became friends almost instantly. I was still healthy then. I invited him to visit us. He spent several months here, as my mother said. We all liked him. Then one day I went out riding and had this… accident. When I needed his help the most, he packed his things and left."

"That is why your mother despises him," I said. "He betrayed you."

"No one here has seen him since then."

"Who introduced you at the party?" asked Holmes.

The young man hesitated before answering.

"The host," he mumbled. "Mr Oscar Wilde."

"Aha, then I understand what kind of party it was," said the detective. "Unfortunately Mr Wilde can no longer tell us where he met your friend."

Holmes was not fond of the popular dramatist. He could not abide his conceited behaviour. Wilde had once even come to us with a request for advice, and it was the most awkward moment in my life. After his death Holmes even rather tactlessly noted that considering his lifestyle it could not have been otherwise.

"You still have not told me why you are looking for him? And why here?"

Holmes briefly summarised the reasons for our investigation. As he spoke the young man turned pale.

"But I am James St. John-Smythe!" he exclaimed in amazement.

"I know," said the detective. "And it is also clear why he so blatantly passed himself off as you. He knows you, knows your parents and circumstances; after all he lived here long enough. He also knows that in all likelihood you will not show up in London and surprise him. He used your name to ingratiate himself with several people, from whom he later stole significant sums of money."

"What should I do?"

"There is nothing you can do. Just help me find him."

"I will do what I can!"

"Then our chances have improved," said Holmes.

He sensed how hard it was for young St. John-Smythe to talk about this man who had so shamefully taken advantage of him and betrayed his affection.

"Did he tell you anything about himself while he was living here?"

"Nothing specific. I know only that he was not an Englishman. He was from the continent."

"Anything else?"

"No, that's all, unfortunately."

The rest of the conversation did not reveal anything of any great import. After a while St. John-Smythe closed himself off from us as though suffering from some inner torture.

We left the cold, empty house and its sad inhabitants and returned to Chiphead.

As we sat in the train to London Holmes suddenly became chatty.

"An interesting case, wouldn't you say?"

"Indubitably," I said, nodding.

The detective nestled even more comfortably into the seat of our compartment. He nibbled inadvertently on the stem of his pipe as he pieced together the various bits of information that we had gathered.

"A young man arrives in England from somewhere on the continent and meets Oscar Wilde who at one of his celebrated parties introduces him as Henry. The man establishes an intimate relationship with young St. John-Smythe and gains his trust. Indeed, he even moves in with him. When the host becomes unexpectedly paralysed he takes advantage of the situation by using his name and reputation to infiltrate high society. He had to act skilfully and make sure to avoid people who knew the real St. John-Smythe. But due to his peculiar inclinations there were not that many of them. He surrounds himself with a circle of new friends, and because it would not even occur to them to doubt his genuineness, they provided him with the base he needed for his other plans, whatever they were. He also had to be sure to avoid any scandal so that his name would not appear in the papers."

"And what about the wedding announcement?"

"He could not influence that. How would he explain it to his new father-in-law? Here he was lucky. He had heard that the old lord had died and apparently nobody else at the estate reads the papers. Lady St. John-Smythe had other matters to concern himself with."

"Doubtless you are correct," I said. "But such a complex plan just for a common marriage fraud? Is it not a little extreme?"

"That was not the only fraud that he perpetrated. He also took advantage of other people and stole money from them."

"Poor Miss Watts! That fraudster must have nerves of steel to lead half of London by the nose like that for a whole year!"

"Clearly he does."

"Do you think he planned it from the start?"

"It depends what you mean by *from the start*. He could not have planned the paralysis."

"Unless he helped it along somehow…"

"That is unlikely," said Holmes. "To cause an accident in such a way that the rider is only paralysed and not killed is practically impossible. He would have to be a truly expert horseman. In my opinion he merely took advantage of the opportunities that presented themselves."

"Such a diabolical idea cannot occur to a decent man out of nowhere!"

"You are certainly right, my friend. Perhaps he originally planned something else, but he definitely did not befriend St. John-Smythe with honest intentions."

"Do you think that's why he came all the way to England?"

"It is still too early to speculate."

"Has the case captured your fancy?" I asked. "Do you intend to pursue it?"

"Yes," Holmes nodded. "The task was clear: find the man. So far we have not succeeded. I believe, however, that it will not take long."

"Where shall we begin the search? He can be hiding anywhere under any alias!"

Holmes yawned and waved his hand.

"We know that he often returned to the continent. Our investigation should continue there. Our may last some time. What do you say, Watson?"

I had not been on the continent in a long time. It might be amusing. I agreed and for the rest of the journey we discussed various aspects of the case. We arrived home shortly after dark, but our work that day was not yet done.

A visitor was waiting for us.

*Watson's second (or third) wife, whom he married on October 4, 1902.
** Mary Morstan, Watson's first (or second) wife.

IV

The Die is Cast

Mr Christopher Watts was an imposing man with a bearing entirely proportionate to his social position. As he stood up from the chair in which he sat in our lodgings I estimated his height at some six feet five inches. Dressed in a fine dark suit and waistcoat and matching cravat he was a perfect image of a successful man. A long cane with a massive head was propped against the coffee table. He stood up when we entered the drawing room, leaning on the cane for support.

"Gentlemen," he said with a slight bow of his head. "I hope that I am not disturbing you."

"Not at all," Holmes replied. "To tell the truth, I have been expecting your visit. I trust you haven't been kept waiting long?"

Visibly exhausted, the guest sat down.

"You know who I am," he said flatly. "Knowing your reputation I should not be surprised. But I am curious to know by what method you arrived at your conclusion."

"It is elementary deduction," said Holmes, shrugging his shoulders. "Nothing that any reasonably clever policeman couldn't do. *Àpropos*, Watson, what do you think? Would you be able to determine the identity of our guest?"

I saw the glimmer in his eyes. He loved to tease my brain. If I learned something over the years spent together it was not to be distracted. Holmes would never intentionally embarrass me; he had to know that even I knew who the guest was.

"But of course!" I said, levelling an examining gaze at the man in the armchair. "One clue is the initials C, H and W, which are etched into the head of your cane. Another hint is the page of yesterday's edition of the *Post* protruding from your pocket, whose headline announces a certain scandal in bold print. Who else would carry an old newspaper in their pocket except perhaps the subject of the report himself?"

"Extraordinary!" said Watts with amazement, while Holmes lifted an eyebrow. "What a keen sense of observation! Clearly you have a fine associate, Mr Holmes."

"Watson's ability to look at problems with the guileless eyes of a man unable to perform an evil act has often proved invaluable to me," said the detective, taking off his coat and sitting in the armchair across from Watts. "Especially when I get carried away and start thinking far beyond the confines of the simple criminal mind. But certainly you are not here just to give us compliments."

The merchant's hand, which until now had been placed calmly on his cane, clutched convulsively, and his cheeks turned purple.

"Indeed, Mr Holmes, you are right as always. As Dr Watson said, I am here because of the article. I wanted to ask you to take on my case and help me find the man who has so shamefully used my daughter."

"I'm already familiar with the circumstances of the case."

The merchant paused, and for the first time during his visit seemed genuinely surprised.

"I'm afraid I don't entirely follow you," he said.

Holmes folded his long fingers together and nodded soberly.

"I trust that I will not be breaking client privilege when I tell you that your daughter has already come to me."

"She said nothing of this to me!"

"That is understandable. While you would like nothing more than to see the young man hanged, she sees it all as an accident and fears for his life."

Watts wiped the sweat from his brow and the tension in his body eased a little. He let go of the cane and leaned back in the chair, but was still breathing hard.

"I know about that," he admitted. "But it cannot be just a coincidence. I lost even more money than Annabelle thinks! And the young man has disappeared without a trace! What do you think about it, Mr Holmes? Am I jumping to conclusions?"

Sharing bad news was no less unpleasant for Holmes than it was for any ordinary mortal, but his cold and detached manner sometimes made it seem otherwise.

"Normally I would only share the results of my investigation with my client," he said."But with regard to the circumstances I can also share them with you. I'm afraid, however, that the findings are unpleasant. You and your daughter have been the victims of an extraordinarily cunning con artist!"

"Indeed! What have you found?"

"The clues point to multiple frauds committed on various people."

"Good God, Mr Holmes, stop keeping me in suspense!"

"In recent days Dr Watson and I have made a number of visits during which we attempted to gather information about Lord St. John-Smythe, as we did not learn too many details from Miss Annabelle," said Holmes not changing the pace at which he revealed the information and continuing on as he considered appropriate.

"That was one of my first objections when she told me about her intention to marry him. She knew nothing about him; they had barely known each other a couple of months. Had I not vetted him I would not even know his first name!"

"Which leads me to the question of how the vetting proceeded?"

"I contacted several of my friends and asked them for a small service."

"And what did you discover?"

"The references for St. John-Smythe's family were excellent! The estate in Surrey is among the largest in the area and together with the lands and forests are worth a staggering amount. The director of the First National Bank, Mr Halworth, told me in confidence that their account may be getting thinner in recent years, but they still have the house and land. The most important thing was that the family's reputation is completely without scandal."

"Which together with the fact that the sole heir to the property and noble title behaved kindly was reason enough for you to accept the match," said Holmes dryly. "Is that not so?"

"You misjudge me, sir," said Watts. "My first priority is my daughter's happiness. To accuse me of being calculating is shameful of you!"

Shamefulness was not something of which one could accuse Sherlock Holmes, and so my friend paused. Nothing could be read from his stern face and so I was surprised when he slapped his knees with amusement and burst out laughing.

"Please continue," he said politely. "What did you do after the unhappy wedding? Why did you wait until only tonight to see me?"

"I was furious," said Watts, confirming what our client had said. "I was overcome by mental and physical exhaustion. Last night even a doctor had to come see me!"

This did not surprise me. The signs of his recent collapse were evident. His breathing, the colour of his face and the weakness in his eyes all pointed to the need for rest. The discoveries that he could make by talking to us might put him in serious danger.

"The doctor ordered me to rest, but I can think of nothing else. My wife persuaded me that seeing you might bring a solution. But now please tell me truly what you have learned!"

"The references did not lie. Lord St. John-Smythe is indeed an honest man. Unfortunately, the man who introduced himself to your daughter under this name is a fraud. The real James St. John-Smythe was crippled some years ago and since then has not shown his face in London. This gave the con man the opportunity to pretend to be him without fear of discovery."

"But I met his parents!" said the duped father, gasping for breath.

"Hired actors. The real Lord St. John-Smythe is dead."

"Good God! When I imagine that he was a guest in my home!"

Watts loosened his shirt collar and asked for a glass of water.

"The shame of it!" he exclaimed.

"Do you have any expensive jewellery or valuables that he might have had access to during his stay?" asked Holmes.

"Why?"

"I have a justified suspicion that among other things he had forgeries made of certain items from your household and switched them for the originals!"

"How do you know?"

"The brooch which Miss Annabelle wore on her wedding day was without doubt a brilliant forgery. By chance it fell into my hands and upon closer inspection I was even able to say with absolute certainty who created the forgery."

"You don't mean–"

"The one that you gave to your wife as an engagement present," said Holmes.

This was new information for me too. My secretive friend had not mentioned it.

Watts turned pale and gasped for breath.

"Quick, Watson, he is having another attack!" cried Holmes, jumping from his chair.

I sprang forward and grasped Watts's wrist.

His pulse was racing.

"Fetch some brandy!"I cried to the detective while I massaged the man's temples.

The detective brought the decanter from the table and poured out a glass. I placed it to the man's mouth and slapped him on the cheeks. A moment later he relaxed and his pulse slowed. But I could not allow Holmes to torture him with more details.

"You need rest. Your heart cannot take more bad news!"

"But what should I do? I can't just leave things as they are."

"Allow me to offer you my services," said Holmes. "I would like to continue the work that your daughter assigned to me."

"Do you have any leads?"

"I think that our man has fled to the continent."

"How do you expect to find him?"

"Please leave that to me. You heard the doctor's orders. I already have a plan to find him."

"Do so and I will pay you handsomely! I want that wretch in chains!"

Holmes went to the bookshelf and took down a timetable for the *Water Line* shipping company.

"My fee will not be excessive," he said. "Nevertheless, a certain amount will be required for expenses. An investigation abroad is always more expensive."

"Whatever it costs!" said Watts reaching for his chequebook and tearing out a cheque. "Fill in the amount yourself!"

"I shall strive not to be wasteful."

"All I ask is that you keep me informed of your progress," said Watts and he stood up to leave.

He leaned against his cane and headed for the door. Outside a private coach was waiting to take him home.

I watched from the window as he got into the coach. As fate would have it, another coach pulled up in front of the house and out stepped Annabelle Watts. As soon as she saw her father's coach she stopped in surprise and called to him. Her father heard her and turned around.

I could not hear what they were saying, and perhaps that was for the best. In the light of the coach lamp the young lady fell to her knees and buried her face in her father's overcoat, shaking with sobs.

"It's a dirty business," said Holmes, who without my knowledge had been watching the scene from behind me.

I turned away from the window sadly and collapsed into an armchair. The fire in the fireplace was dying out, so Holmes lit a lamp. The yellow light illuminated the cosy salon, cluttered with investigative tools, tubes, alembics, torches, newspapers and various esoteric books.

I rubbed my eyes and walked to the door to go to my bedroom.

"You're not going to sleep are you?" said Holmes, who was leaning against the mantel and lighting a cigar, said to me

"That was indeed intention."

"I was hoping that you would give me another hour or two of your time," he said.

"It's been a long day," I said, and blinked sleepily. "Can't it wait till morning?"

"Night is the best time for my plans," said Holmes. "The people I want to visit are not much out during the day."

In anticipation of the night adventures my tiredness suddenly fell away.

"What sort of expedition are we going on?"

"You must create a diversion so that I can break into the office of a certain jeweller."

"You haven't gone criminal have you!"

"Not at all," he said, laughing. "This jeweller is my old friend, so to speak. Some time ago I sent him to prison for a couple of years, but he is the best forger in London. I recognised his work on that brooch. He might know something about the person who had it made."

"Very well, I shall go get changed."

"That is not necessary," he said, stopping me. "Your clothes are most suitable for this occasion. It is perfect for your role. Instead, I shall go get changed!"

He extinguished his cigar and disappeared behind the doors of his room only to return a moment later ready for our expedition. He wore a greenish jacket and breeches with high knee socks. These clothes allowed him greater freedom of motion for the agile tasks he was no doubt contemplating.

"Watson, bring your revolver," he said. "Just in case."

We walked out into the dark street. A chill wind was blowing, which did not bother me, bundled as I was in my warm coat, but Holmes soon was shivering with cold.

"A coat would only get in my way," he explained. "We must hope it will not take long!"

Thankfully it was warmer in the coach. I didn't hear the address that Holmes barked to the driver. I watched through the fogged up windows as we drew further away from our lodgings in the direction of the Tower Bridge. We crossed it and headed towards a distant part of town, known for its poverty and crime. Our coach was the only one in the area and I prayed that the driver would be willing to wait for us.

We stopped in front of a two-storey house surrounded by a badly kept garden.

"I shall exit from the other side in case someone is watching from the house," said Holmes, and he quickly jumped out and vanished into the hazy darkness.

I also got out and walked through the gate with its creaking hinges. There was a dim light shining from the ground floor of the house, which cast ominous shadows on the garden. The windows along the first and second floors were barred, but not on the upstairs floor. A massive elm grew near the north wall of the house. I assumed that Holmes would use it to climb into the upper part of the house.

I felt the revolver in my pocket. I had owned it ever since my military service and it had often served me and Holmes well. Feeling reassured I boldly knocked on the door of the house.

Several long passed and then I heard shuffling steps on the other side. The peephole slid open and an eye stared at me.

"Are you Mr Terry Thorpe?" I asked.

"What do you want?" said a hoarse voice. "Who are you?"

"Henry sent me!" I answered, just as Holmes had instructed.

The eye for a moment looked at me suspiciously. Then it disappeared and the lock clicked. The door opened about halfway and I was beckoned inside.

In a small dark hallway, pervaded by an unknown smell, stood a man who despite not being so old was hunched over like a centenarian. He wore thick glasses, through which he stared at me sullenly. Unshaven, with large grey whiskers on his face and dressed in a tattered robe, he reminded me of Ebenezer Scrooge.

"What do you want?" he grumbled.

I coughed, as though it was embarrassing for me to talk about it, and nervously squeezed the revolver in my pocket.

"I... uh, that is, I have found myself in a rather difficult financial situation and I will be forced to sell some of the family jewellery."

"This isn't a pawnshop."

"No, of course not. My request is of a more, um, delicate nature. I cannot let my wife or her family know about my, ahem, situation. What I would like to ask you is whether you could make a copy for me of several pieces. Not too expensive copies."

Thorpe squinted at me suspiciously.

"The races," I continued."Fortune has not been kind to me lately."

"What a foolish reason to become impoverished," he said.

"I will get my money back, I just need a little time," I continued. "But I have the money to pay for your work!"

"Very well, because of Henry I will accept your order," he growled. "But you'll have to be patient!"

He returned to the door and locked it with a heavy bolt. Then he motioned to me to follow him and led me down a groaning wooden staircase to the basement. I walked carefully behind him, my mind racing. Holmes had not given me instructions for what to do next. My original assumption had been that as soon as Holmes was inside the house or had finished doing what he needed to do he would give me some sort of signal.

We entered a spacious underground chamber, where I could smell turpentine and some other substances that I could not identify. Thorpe lit the lamp and sat at a desk covered with scrap, ferrous metals, slides and delicate tools. He took off his glasses, put a magnifying glass on his left eye, and held out his skinny hand in expectation.

"Show me your treasures."

That was a problem. Besides my wedding band I of course had no jewellery with me and I began to panic. The only thing I could do was pull out my revolver and hold the man at bay until Holmes appeared.

"That won't be necessary, Watson," said the detective as though reading my mind and he stepped from out of a dark corner of the workshop. "If our friend should call the police it would look like an armed robbery!"

Thorpe gasped and the magnifying glass fell with a loud thud on the table.

"So, we meet again, Terry," said Holmes.

Then his features hardened and quick as a cat he sprang on him. He grabbed the man's thin arm and tore away the pistol which Thorpe had concealed under the table.

"Always ready, isn't that so?" said the detective, putting the pistol in his pocket and letting go of Thorpe's arm with repulsion.

"What do you want?" cried the forger. "I haven't done anything!"

"That depends on you," said Holmes. "Either you cooperate with me or I will take you to the station."

"You've got nothing on me!"

My friend looked at the desk and opened one of the drawers. He had used the time I had given him to search the workshop and now he knew exactly where to go. He reached into the drawer and pulled out a ring.

"This no doubt belongs to a certain Lady Starling."

The hunched man grimaced.

"You're a dirty cop, Holmes!"

"We all have to make a living," said Holmes, shrugging. "Today my fee depends on whether I can find a certain man. I think you can help me."

"I know lots of people!"

"About five months ago this man asked you to forge a very valuable brooch."

"I receive many such orders."

"He called himself Henry."

"I don't know him."

"Come now. After all, my friend used his name to get in."

Thorpe spat.

"I want to know how many copies you made for him and why."

"I don't know him!" said the jeweller.

Holmes brought his face right next to Thorpe's.

"Do not try my patience," he said menacingly."I know that nobody gets to you without excellent references. Tell me who it was or you go back to jail!"

"I don't know his full name," said the jeweller. "Mayer sent him here! He had a letter from him."

"What was in it?"

"He vouched for him. I was to do all that he asked."

"And what did you do?"

"I made a few copies of various items, mostly jewellery. All in three months. He hasn't been here since then, I swear!"

"Where is the list?"

"There, in that drawer."

Holmes dug around in the drawer that Thorpe had pointed to and found a ripped piece of paper with notes.

"I am inclined to believe you this time, Terry. But I must warn you to choose your customers more carefully. Otherwise we will meet again. The next time it might not go so well for you."

He looked around the dark workshop.

"Let's go, Watson," he said nodding to me.

I left the room first and Holmes joined me on the staircase. He urged me to make haste, constantly looking behind him.

"Quickly, while he is still confused! I would not like to stay in this house a moment longer than necessary. I have no doubt that the gun under the table was not the only surprise he has for unwanted guests."

We left the house and walked swiftly to the metal gate, behind which fortunately for us the coach was still waiting. The considerably coachman was numb with cold.

"You must always insist on paying only upon the return journey," said Holmes as he sat down.

He slammed the door of the coach and I finally caught my breath.

"Holmes, it was getting pretty hot in there before you turned up," I said.

"You played it brilliantly! And now we have another clue that points to the old continent!"

"Mayer?"

"The head of the Austro-Hungarian underworld. A very powerful man. And a dreaded adversary, whom the local police have yet to apprehend. If he has any connection with our fraudster, we can catch two birds with one stone!"

"So off to Europe then!" I cried, suddenly full of enthusiasm.

"Yes, Watson, tomorrow we set off on our journey," said the detective, lighting yet another cigar. *"Alea iacta est*!"

* The die is cast! Julius Caesar's words when he crossed the Rubicon in 49 AD.

V

The French Noblewoman's Diamonds

The morning after our night's adventure saw us preparing for our journey. As Holmes quipped, nothing happened during that time that was worthy of a story in the *Strand*. This comment did not offend me, for I knew with what interest and even smug satisfaction he followed my literary accounts of his genius.

While I was in charge of arranging our tickets for the journey, Holmes again visited our clients, who were connected by a desire to apprehend the fake St. John-Smythe, and informed them of the latest developments in the investigation. This fellowship now consisted of Mr Gottfried and Mr Watts, as well as the jilted Annabelle Watts.

In the hours before our departure, however, Holmes had another small matter to deal with. Mr Watts had identified several more items in his house that proved to be forgeries and had suffered another breakdown. But in the end this event only served to strengthen our client's resolve.

Shortly after noon on the fourth of October we found ourselves in a coach speeding towards Victoria Station, where the train to Dover was waiting for us. As soon as the locomotive lurched forward and the wagons were set in motion, Holmes nestled his head in the soft headrest with the intention of catching up on his sleep.

"What will be our first stop?"

"Ask the conductor," he yawned without opening his eyes.

"Does he know so much about our investigation?"

"Oh, that's what you meant. In that case my answer will be different. Paris, naturally."

Ah, I thought, the city of light!

"Unfortunately we will not have time to see the sights," said Holmes, again reading my thoughts as though they were imprinted on my forehead.

He stretched out his long legs and opened a French textbook. He licked his finger and turned the pages.

"We have a lot of work ahead of us going through local police records," he said dryly.

"Do you hope to find something there about our man?"

"Thanks to the dedicated efforts of young Bertillon I believe so, yes. Such an experienced fraudster with contacts in the European underworld should have a fairly thorough record!"

"Aren't such contacts a little strange?"

"My dear Watson!" he said laughing. "Much has changed since the Franco-Prussian War! The borders between the criminal organisations of Germany, France and Austria-Hungary are not as clearly defined as those between their fractious rulers. Crime, Watson, is one big family!"

"But what if the police refuse to let you access their records?"

"The Sûreté owes me at least this favour. The local chief of police will no doubt be glad to show off the archive that he has so painstakingly built!"

"Perhaps you are right," I said. "But I am still not entirely convinced that a few anthropological measurements can reliably identify a man."

"I myself did not pay attention to these observations," said Holmes, placing a finger in the book and crossing one leg over the other. "Truth be told, I also have certain doubts about Bertillonage*. But at least we can use it as a guide. As yet we have nothing better! Even though I place great hope in dactiloscopy!"

"That has to do with fingerprints, right?"

"Yes. This science is based on the assumption that the papillary lines on the palms and on the balls of the fingers are different for each person. According to Galton**no two people have the same prints. They have been using it for some time in America and are having a great deal of success with it. We shall see if it has a future!"

With that he returned to his French lessons.

Dover welcomed us with its hustle and bustle as well as fog, through which we could not see farther than a few yards. In the port itself it was even thicker, but I will never forget the view of the massive hulls of the ships that emerged before us. Holmes paid the coachman and I waited on the pier with our luggage until he brought our boarding passes.

I spent the time inspecting the ship that was to take us to Calais. The faded grey hull did not inspire much confidence. I found it amusing that the hulk was called *The Sprinter*.

Suddenly someone shoved me rudely from behind. It was the servant of a young lady, carrying many large pieces of luggage in his arms, which entirely blocked his view. Upon colliding with me he dropped some of them, but the maid, who formed the second part of the retinue, helped him pick them up again.

"*Excusez moi*," said their employer, apologising profusely. "I hope you are all right?"

I regained my composure and nodded.

"I'm afraid is what happens when you hire servants just for the season," she continued in a charming French accent. "The best are just not to be had."

She was a beautiful and slender young woman, radiant with energy and the joy of life. Her curly copper-coloured hair was bunched under a wide-brimmed hat decorated with a lace veil, behind which shone blue eyes and perfectly sculpted lips. A dark scarf covered the elegant curve of her neck, and fell over her stylish suit with its long skirt, cut according to the latest French fashion. A tiny hand extended from a fur muff.

I assured her of my indestructibility and took the proffered, surprisingly firm hand, and kissed it gallantly. As my lips approached, I detected a subtle scent, sweet and still fresh, such as can only be produced in one country on Earth.

"English gentlemen are so attentive and polite," she smiled kindly. "But our men catch up with their charm and sensuality!"

"What has led you to conclude that Englishmen are so cold?"

"A too intimate question from an unknown man," she replied wickedly. "Mr ...?"

"Forgive me," I said, doffing my hat. "My name is John H. Watson, doctor of medicine."

"Pleased to make your acquaintance. I am Marie Framboise, the Countess d'Ambolieu."

We shook hands, and since her company was pleasant to me, I continued our conversation.

"Were you visiting a friend in England or did you come here to see its beauties?"I asked amiably.

"I came to invite a friend to a wedding, and my fiancé is a Frenchman, a native of Paris, thus my comment about English reserve," she added conspiratorially.

I did not feel it appropriate to argue with her patriotic convictions, so I shifted the conversation to other, less thorny topics.

"Are you travelling alone?"

"Yes, just with me retinue. And what about you? What important matter has ripped you away from your wife and a warm fire to cross the cold Channel?"

"Business in Paris," I said quickly. "I am meeting a colleague there."

"Perhaps we shall meet again during the crossing," she said by way of goodbye. "I look forward to your introducing me to your companion."

She nodded her head gracefully and left. Her servants meanwhile had boarded and she followed them up the wooden boarding ramp holding lightly to the swinging railing. I watched her slender silhouette through the haze as she disappeared among the people aboard ship. But now Holmes was returning and he pressed a boarding pass into my hand.

"We cast off in a few minutes," he informed me. "Let us board."

He took up our light bags and we immediately stepped aboard *The Sprinter*.

In a few minutes the ship's horn sounded and from the cabin porthole I could see the slowly receding dock with its moored barges, boats, clippers and schooners.

"We have to prepare for a tedious two-hour voyage," said Holmes.

Fortunately soon after our departure the haze cleared and the sun began to shine. Its rays reflected on the silver crests of the waves with such brightness that they tempted me out to walk about the deck and I left Holmes without regret to his book.

Apparently I was not the only one who did not want to spend the voyage enclosed in a small cabin. The upper deck was crawling with people.

I leant on the railing for about half an hour savouring the fresh air and counting the seagulls circling in the distance over the receding Dover.

The idyll was interrupted by angry shouting.

It came from the bow, where the first-class cabins were located. I ran in the direction of the commotion and when I arrived a small group of people had gathered in front of the door of one of the cabins. Inside I could hear cursing, and even though I did not understand the language, it was obviously quite colourful. Then the doors flew open with a bang and the Countess d'Ambolieu stormed out.

Her eyes flashed lightning, her lips were pressed together in a solid line, and with a vigorous movement she shooed away the curious bystanders. Shouting angrily she marched towards the bridge. I scurried after her, ready to offer my help, but she was already banging on the captain's door.

It was opened by a hulk of a man in a white uniform. His steel-grey eyes suggested that he did not take kindly to the interruption.

"Whoa, ma'am!" he roared. "Is there a fire?"

"How dare you talk to me like that!" said the lady pompously. "Do you know who I am?"

"I don't care if you're Joan of Arc; I am the master of this boat," the captain boomed. "Try again – and politely this time!"

And he slammed the door in her face.

She stared aghast for a moment. I had no doubt that her knocking would eventually rip the door to shreds, and therefore I intervened in order to prevent a potentially ugly confrontation.

"May I help you in any way?"I offered from a safe distance.

"Ah, Dr Watson," she said, attempting a smile. "I surely did not imagine our second meeting this way. But perhaps you can help me with this oaf!"

"Has something happened?"

The Countess tried to calm herself by breathing slowly.

"Yes, something has happened," she said icily. "There is a thief among the crew!"

"Are you certain?"

The look that I received in response to my innocent question was one that I would not wish on my worst enemy.

"Quite!" she barked and turned her attention back to the door.

"In that case, perhaps I could ask my friend to look into your problem. I believe that no one on board is better suited to this matter."

"And who is your friend?" she grumbled. "Auguste Dupin***?"

"Not at all," I protested."It is Sherlock Holmes!"

"I don't know him," she muttered between her teeth. "I don't see how he can help me."

"Then at least let me take care of this matter," I said placing myself between her and the door, and before she could protest I knocked politely.

"That's the way to do it!" said the captain stepping from the bridge with a broad grin on his tanned face. "What's on your mind, madam?"

The Countess thrust out her chest proudly.

"A suitcase with my personal jewellery was taken from my cabin! I ask that the ship refrain from docking before the thief is found!"

"The request is denied," said the captain. "There are a hundred and fifty people on this ship who would throw me over the side if they did not arrive in time."

"You're covering for someone in the crew!" she hissed, stabbing her tiny index finger into the man's enormous chest. "I shall file a complaint about you!"

The captain did not expect this.

"Madam, I must protest!" he said."The sailors on this ship may be old men, but their honesty is above reproach!"

The Countess looked over his shoulder at the bridge as though a phantom was hiding there and shot an accusatory look at the helmsman.

"And what should I do according to you?"

"When we land at Calais go to the nearest police station."

"By the time I come back with the police everyone will be gone!"

"There is nothing I can do," said the captain. "I can't keep these people here!"

"How long before we arrive?"

"Half an hour if the current is favourable."

The Countess sighed with exasperation and turned her back on the captain of *The Sprinter*.

"Come, doctor. Introduce me to your friend!"

* * *

I led the Countess to our cabin on deck B. Along the way she told me that these kinds of things always excite her and that she once had a similar thing happen to her on the Orient Express, but that fortunately it had been resolved.

Before she could finish telling me her story we were standing before Holmes.

He snapped shut his book and raised an inquisitive eyebrow.

"I can't leave you alone for a moment..." he said under his breath when he saw the attractive woman who was with me.

As a married man I politely skipped over his comment and introduced him to the Countess.

"*Bonjour, madame.* It is a poor day for such a cold voyage, is it not?" Holmes said to her in perfect French.

"*Oh, oui!*" she said with delight. "Where did you learn to speak French so well?"

"I have visited your country several times. Unfortunately, always in a professional capacity."

"Yes, Dr Watson already mentioned it."

"If yes, then he has already revealed several state secrets!"he said, switching back to English.

The lady laughed, thinking it was a joke, but then her face immediately became troubled again.

"I do not even know why I am bothering you, but Dr Watson insists that I must confide in you."

"Please continue," said Holmes. "Perhaps I can be of some assistance."

"I have no better alternative," she said resignedly.

My friend, who was used to clients seeking his help in the first order and not as a last resort, offered her a chair and asked her to tell him what happened.

"When I boarded and stored my luggage I was tempted outside by the improved weather. I locked up the room and left the only key with my chambermaid, who was with me the whole time. We spent some time on deck when my servant came looking for me to say that there were strange noises coming from our cabin. I returned immediately and found my things all tossed about. The little suitcase with my jewellery had been prised opened and my diamonds were missing! But the door to the cabin was undamaged!"

"Did you inform the captain?"

"Of course! I am to go to the police when we arrive, but by then the thief and my jewels will be long gone!"

"We will arrive in half an hour," said the detective, glancing out the window. "We have a lot to do! First I would like to see the scene of the crime."

"You are a true gentleman, unlike that oaf in uniform!" she cried and glided out the door, trusting that we would follow her.

Holmes also stood up and threw his cloak over his shoulders. I was expecting him to ask me whether I had said anything about the purpose of our journey, but he interrupted me.

"I understand why you are so enchanted with her. She does not lack a certain charm and sensuality, of which her countrywomen are justly famous. Never mind the fact that she bears a certain resemblance to Miss Morstan."

This was a reminder of my beloved wife. I went after him, momentarily overwhelmed by memories. Holmes did not delay and immediately entered the cabin in which the Countess was already waiting for him with the chambermaid and the servant. Also present was the captain, perhaps as a sign of goodwill. He made a great show of ignoring the Countess and welcomed both of us profusely.

The detective did not bother with pleasantries, and immediately walked around the cabin. He also looked out the small porthole and thoughtfully at the items that were scattered about.

"Everything was as it is now?"

"Yes, Mr Holmes, I did not touch a thing. I only picked up the little suitcase."

I looked around but did not see the little suitcase anywhere. Neither did Holmes.

"And where is the little suitcase?"

The lady exhaled defiantly.

"I tossed it somewhere. It must be under the cabinet."

"Here it is!" said my friend, pulling out a red velvet-covered jewellery box.

"Yes, as you said, it's been prised open," he said, examining the lock. "The scratches suggest a knife with several teeth, the kind used by sailors."

"It was none of my men!" said the captain.

"Are you certain about all of them to a man?"

"Yes! They are honest men! They might slap someone about or get into a pub brawl, but they would never rob our passengers!"

"For the time being I do not accuse them either. The manner in which the theft was carried outdoes not suggest it."

"Could it have been one of the passengers?" cried the lady.

The detective inhaled and took a few deliberate steps around the small cluster of people gathered in the cabin. His hands, folded as they were behind his back, indicated that he was thinking. But it was not a hard nut for him to crack.

"The manner and position of the things thrown about the cabin indicates that this was only a cover-up designed to point the finger at a crewmember, as was the use of the knife," he said. "The thief knew exactly what he was looking for and where to go!"

"But only I and the servants knew about the jewels! The key was with the chambermaid, who was with me the whole time, and the servant does not have one! As the doors were not prised open it must have been someone from the crew, someone with a spare key! The steward!"

"I am the only one with a universal key," said the captain.

Holmes shook his head vigorously. He again circled the small party, this time in the opposite direction, and stopped in front of the young chambermaid.

"What is your name, dear?"

"Emma West, sir," she said, blinking.

"Emma," he said to her in a friendly tone. "You were with your mistress the whole time?"

"Yes!"

"I can testify to that," said the Countess.

"You had the key on your person?"

"Yes, in my pocket!"

"Really?"

"Certainly!" she cried, but she turned away her eyes.

That was enough for Holmes. He threw up his hands and turned to the others.

"I am afraid, Countess, that your chambermaid is lying!" he said. "She gave the key to her accomplice, who then easily stole your jewels!"

"But to whom?"

"The accomplice can be none other than your servant," he said, pointing at the man who had bumped into me on the dock. "During the crush to board he stealthily approached and got the key from the chambermaid. He returned it to her when he came to inform you about the supposed robbery!"

The pair of suspects huddled close together, their gazes fixed on the ground.

"I dare say that if you search this gentleman you will find your jewels!"

The captain put his large hand on the culprit's shoulder and told him to turn his pockets inside out. When the servant failed to comply, the captain did it himself and pulled out of his pocket two beautiful diamond earrings. The maid was sobbing. The Countess looked as though she might slap her. Then she controlled herself and only coldly repeated what she had already told me on the dock.

"I will never again hire servants just for the season! But there is one piece still missing," she added, frowning. "A diamond medallion!"

Holmes reached into the thief's other pocket and a large diamond, which was clearly from the same collection, sparkled in the light. As he removed it the latch caught the hem of the servant's pocket and the locket opened. The detective glanced at the picture inside, and handed the medallion back to the happy owner.

"I don't know how to thank you, Mr Holmes!"

"My reward is the satisfaction that I have again helped the cause of justice," he said bowing. "I would second the advice that next time you make a better choice of your retinue."

"I too would like to thank you," said the captain, shaking Holmes's hand. "You removed all suspicion from my men!"

The captain then led the culprits onto the deck.

"Dr Watson told me that you have a meeting in Paris," said the Countess, caressing her favourite jewel affectionately. "We are going the same way. Allow me to invite you to dinner as a sign of my gratitude. I would also like to take the opportunity to introduce you to my fiancé. Among other things, I received this collection from him."

Although my friend usually refused such invitations, I noted with surprise that this time he accepted.

By now we were so close to the harbour that we could hear the cries of seagulls. The ship lurched and stopped, reminding me that this time I had completely forgotten to succumb to seasickness.

Holmes and I went to pick up our luggage. We again met the Countess at the exit ramp. At the captain's orders one of the sailors was helping her with her luggage and accompanied her all the way to her carriage. We also disembarked, and were rewarded with an honorary salute from the crew, who were lined up on deck under the supervision of the captain himself.

In the end we also had the pleasure of the Countess's refreshing presence in the train to Paris and at her recommendation we stayed in the same hotel as her, *Le Renaissance*, located on one of Paris's grandest boulevards.

We announced ourselves at the reception desk and a bellboy immediately took us to our rooms.

Within an hour we were dressed for dinner and we met the Countess in the lobby at the entrance to the restaurant.

We were about to meet her fiancé.

*Bertillonage– an identification method of determining a person by means of eleven anthropological measurements, named after its creator, the police officer Alphonse Bertillon (1863–1914).
**Francis Galton (1822– 1911) – a scientist who demonstrated the individuality and permanence of papillary ridges and promoted the use of fingerprinting in forensics.
*** We know that Holmes was not especially impressed by this literary predecessor of his, who for instance solved the murder in the Rue Morgue.

VI

Face to Face

We traversed a luxurious red carpet into the high-ceilinged salon of the *Renaissance Soir* restaurant, admiring its lavish furnishings and the two large palm trees at the entrance. As soon as we stepped inside we were met by a tall head waiter in a tailcoat and starched shirtfront. His reserved manner and icy expression soon gave way to a delighted smile when he recognised our companion, the Countess.

He immediately led us through a spacious aisle between the tables. We walked past huge round tables, set with snow white tablecloths and baskets of flowers. The room was lit by crystal chandeliers, their white light reflecting on the silverware and dishes. One wall of the restaurant was completely glass, through which one could see the street full of people walking by. In the corner there was a piano on a raised podium on which a thin young man played various pleasant melodies whose sound blended with the tinkling of glasses and the hum of conversation.

The Countess's fiancé was sitting at the table. When he saw us he stood up and smoothed his thin moustache with his finger, which sported an immense ring. Our companion kissed him.

Before us was the man from Lady Watts's photograph. The vein on my temple began to pulse with anger. His haircut and facial hair were different, but it was clearly him. I wanted to tear this kind woman from his arms and pull the mask off this vile charlatan. I glanced at Holmes to gauge his reaction, but he smiled at the couple with complete impartiality.

"This time fate has dealt us a most favourable hand, Watson," he whispered to me out of the corner of his mouth.

I could see, however, that he was not the least bit surprised.

"How did you do it?"I gulped. "Did you arrange this?"

"No, Watson, life itself has arranged it. But to be honest I am not surprised. Did you see how those gems we found glistened? Real ones never shine as bright. These are more of Thorpe's fakes."

"What will we do?"

"For now nothing," he whispered. "I shall not squander the opportunity to study his behaviour up close. Perhaps he will unwittingly reveal something about his diabolically twisted plans!"

"Darling," the Countess said, taking her fiancé by the arm."Allow me to introduce these two gentlemen from England –Mr Holmes and Dr Watson. And this darling man is my fiancé, monsieur Jacques Prosac!"

I shook the man's hand, but I had to force myself to smile. Even his handshake seemed slimy and insincere. We took our seats around the table. I sat between Holmes and the Countess, directly opposite the impostor.

Mr Prosac, or so he called himself, ordered champagne. He had a gracious social manner, and I noticed that the eyes of the women in the room often darted in his direction. I did not understand the attraction. Perhaps it was his dark, exotic skin tone, expressive eyes and eyebrows and affected airs. But his most conspicuous feature was an enlarged lower lip, which made him seem brazen and defiant.

Before inspecting the menu we conversed for a little while. Prosac replied rather vaguely to Holmes's questions about his work and past.

How could the Countess be so blind?

When they brought our dinner, an excellent guinea fowl with cream sauce, she recounted the story of what had happened aboard *The Sprinter*.

"These gentlemen were so terrific, especially Dr Watson, when that awful captain refused to help me!" she said, while he listened with a cold smile and drank Cuvée Dom Pérignon. "And then what Mr Holmes did was truly phenomenal! You could make a living doing that!"

Holmes smiled humbly.

"In fact, that *is* what I do," he said.

"Marie told me that you are businessmen," Prosac said, oblivious to the fact that the noose was tightening around his neck. "She did not say that you were a detective. I have always wished to meet someone like you. There is something so exciting about fighting crime!"

"Indeed?" said Holmes. "I am happy to hear it."

"I have always admired that famous detective of yours, what is his name…"

"Sherlock Holmes?" I suggested.

"Yes, him!" he said brightly. "You see, I had no idea that I was sitting at the table with his namesake. People must be always getting you two mixed up! That must be entertaining, no?"

"Not particularly," said the detective.

"I was thrilled when I read about his adventures, for instance the one with Gloria Scott! But I heard that he recently became a cocaine addict. What a pity."

I froze and Holmes lowered his gaze.

The Countess laughed and nestled in her fiancé's arm.

"Darling! What are you saying? They are just teasing you. Mr Holmes is indeed named Sherlock, and although I had never heard of him before today, he is indeed a brilliant detective!"

Prosac smiled stiffly, but otherwise mastered his emotions impressively. He did not reveal the slightest concern and only coughed lightly.

The pianist continued to play. Holmes meanwhile ordered another bottle of champagne and that gave the imposter time to regain his composure. Despite the coincidence of our meeting, he had no reason to suspect that we were in Paris because of him and that we knew his real identity.

We continued our meal, chatting about this and that. We discussed politics and even found common ground on the issue of Russia.

Prosac meanwhile seemed increasingly comfortable, which was perhaps why after several minutes he turned to Holmes boldly and asked what brought him to France.

The detective calmly swallowed what he was chewing and looked at him indifferently.

"The doctor and I are on the trail of a con artist."

"Ooh, how exciting!" cried the Countess, who had been bored by the conversation up to now. "Please tell us about it. We are frightfully curious, aren't we darling?"

"A thief?" asked her fiancé.

"Not at all," said Holmes, shaking his head. "It is a most singular case. We are tracking a marriage fraudster!"

Prosac took a long sip from his glass. He slowly wiped his lips with a napkin and folded it next to him on the table.

"Indeed? Your client must be a highly placed figure, is that not so?" he said carefully. "You would not leave England because of some goose."

"She is a very kind woman whose father is a well-known English businessman," said Holmes coldly. "And his daughter is certainly not a goose."

"Jacques often travels across the Channel on business, perhaps he knows her father!" said the Countess excitedly. "Please tell us his name, we are so curious!"

"I don't think we would know each other," Prosac mumbled, pushing his plate away. He was clearly becoming uncomfortable.

"I never reveal the names of my clients, madam," said the detective apologetically.

"Please!" the Countess begged.

"Darling, you cannot ask such things," said her fiancé.

"But I can tell you, confidentially of course," said Holmes smiling.

"We cannot ask you –"

"His name is Mr Christopher Watts and his daughter was the victim of this cunning man."

It was deathly quiet for a moment. The Countess looked at her fiancé, but he had turned his head away.

"Unfortunately, I never had the honour..."

"What a pity," said the noblewoman shrugging her shoulders. "I would like to know what a duped father looks like! It would never happen to me. I have an instinct for people; I would spot a con artist a mile away!"

Holmes wanted to say something but then changed his mind.

"It is not always easy," he said. "They may sometimes hide behind very persuasive masks and lure even the most cautious of us!"

"Not me!"

"I have a photograph that the client gave me," said Holmes. "I will show it to you and you will tell me your opinion."

"Wonderful!"

Prosac wiped his brow. I watched with relish as the ground fell out from beneath his feet and his eyes cast about wildly.

Holmes dug in his pocket and pretended to look for the photograph. I knew that he had it upstairs in the room, but it was interesting to watch whether Prosac's nerves would hold up. The game of cat and mouse was interrupted by the Countess when she looked at her fiancé.

"Darling, are you all right?" she cried. "You are sweating!"

"I feel ill. It's probably the food..."

He adjusted his necktie and loosened the collar of his shirt. "Please excuse me for a moment."

He got up from the table and walked into the aisle in the direction of the bathroom. We watched him go, the Countess with concern for his health, Holmes and I with curiosity.

The detective also stood up.

"Excuse me, I shall be right back," he said to the Countess. "I shall leave you now in the excellent company of Dr Watson."

The noble woman nodded, but she continued to look with concern in the direction of the bathroom door. I attempted to distract her with a tale of one of our adventures, but my efforts proved insufficient.

Five minutes later Prosac burst out of the bathroom and scurried through the aisle in the direction of the exit. He waved to the Countess that everything was all right but it was evident that he was terrified. I did not know what to do and felt momentarily paralysed.

Suddenly Holmes staggered out of the bathroom. He was holding the top of his head and had to lean against the wall for support. Then, seeing the enemy escaping, he shook his head and straightened.

"Catch him, Watson, quickly!"

Prosac heard him as did the other diners and staff. Everyone froze and began looking around. The fraudster took advantage of the moment of surprise and before I could move lunged at the waiter who was blocking his path, knocking him over and sending the meal he was serving flying. The food landed on the décolleté of a fat woman, who protested loudly. Prosac grabbed the fallen silver tray and hurled it straight at Holmes.

It whistled through the air with terrifying speed right above the heads of the seated diners and smashed into the wall directly behind Holmes, narrowly missing the ducking detective. He raised his head and bounded after Prosac.

By then I was on my feet too and the head waiter and a large man from reception were blocking the door.

Most of the exits were thus closed off and our villain had nowhere to run. The guests rose and shouted angrily, creating confusion and giving Prosac time to think. He ran towards the double doors leading to the kitchen. He burst through them just as Holmes and I met in the aisle.

"Quickly, after him!" Holmes cried.

I turned to look at the Countess, who was in shock. Several waiters were fanning her with napkins.

I did not see more because Holmes grabbed me by the wrist and pulled me into the kitchen.

The kitchen was full of steam and packed with cook staff. Above the largest puttering cast-iron stoves rippled fume hoods across the ceiling.

"Which way now?" I asked Holmes.

He looked around and considered. Suddenly, somewhere in front of us came the sound of broken dishes and an angry voice.

"This way! He went through the back door!"

He led me to an iron door through which we exited into a back alley full of trash bins. The alley was long and dark, illuminated only by the light reflected from the nearby streets.

On one side of the alley a suspicious shadow was mounting a bicycle.

"There he is! He's stealing someone's bicycle!"

We ran after him, stumbling and kicking through bags of trash.

The street leading behind the restaurant was one of the many narrow roads that weave through Paris. It was paved in cobblestone and lit only by a few lamps. Thanks to his bicycle Prosac had gained several dozen yards on us, but we were still able to see him across the half-empty street.

"Stop!" Holmes cried, but he doubtless knew it was futile. Pedestrians turned in alarm but could not help. Prosac also glanced over his shoulder, just long enough to lose sight of where he was going, and collided with a slow-moving carriage.

Nobody was hurt, but the crash punctured the front wheel of Prosac's bicycle. He got up and tossed aside the twisted vehicle.

Holmes and I ran toward him.

Prosac did not hesitate. He pushed away the coachman who was trying to help him and jumped into the coachbox. He jerked the reins and the horse began to trot. The coachman cursed and ran after him but the carriage had picked up speed and it was no use.

Perhaps this is where it would have ended had Holmes been capable of accepting defeat. Instead, he looked around quickly and spied a rickety wagon pulled by a pair of tired-looking geldings. It was being driven by a scrawny farmer, probably on his way home from market and the wagon was empty save for a few crates of cabbage.

Alas there was no alternative. The detective stepped into the middle of the road and held up his hand. The wagon stopped in surprise.

"Police!" cried Holmes. "I am commandeering your wagon!"

In a daze the farmer climbed down. Had we given him time, perhaps he would have reconsidered our request, but he just handed us the reins. Sherlock Holmes's powerful personality was hard to resist.

He threw off his tailcoat and we jumped into the wagon and set off.

Our horses seemed to have rediscovered some long-forgotten ancestral heritage and broke into a rapid gallop. The wheels of the wagon bounced violently on the cobblestones and with each bound I feared that they might fly off their axle.

"Can we catch him?" I cried, firmly clutching the handle.

"We have a chance," said Holmes, staring straight ahead. "He might have a better horse, but we have two. And we are lighter!"

We raced at breakneck speed, the night wind whistling past our ears. The streets were filled with bicycles, carts and carriages. Holmes manoeuvred through them brilliantly and inch by inch we gained on Prosac.

We circled the Arc de Triomphe and raced through the brightly lit streets along the eastern side, crossing a wide boulevard and heading towards Avenue de la Grande Armée. People screamed and darted aside when they heard the thunderous clatter of hooves and the rattling wagon. I had to hold on for dear life to keep from falling.

The houses that we were now passing were more opulent and ornate. There were fewer pedestrians now, but our chase did not let up. The horses could not maintain this pace much longer, but Holmes urged them forward. His eyes blazed and his lips were pressed together tightly.

We were getting nearer and nearer to our prey, but there was still a lot of ground left to cover. Our horses' coats glistened with sweat and their heads were starting to sag.

"We need to be lighter!" Holmes cried.

He nodded to the back of the wagon where the crates of cabbage were bouncing. I understood what he wanted and groped my way to the crates. I clung to the railing and crawled back. My hair blew in the wind and my tie whipped across my face. Eventually I got to the crates unscathed and kicked them off the wagon one after another. Countless heads of white cabbage rolled and bounded out onto the street behind us and into the gardens of the white villas.

Lightening the wagon helped us. Now Prosac was almost within our grasp. By the time I re-joined Holmes at the front of the wagon we were already almost level with Prosac's carriage. Our horses were only a few heads behind. We could see Prosac frantically whipping his steed.

He saw us from the corner of his eyes and lashed out at us with his whip. The tip of the whip cracked an inch from my nose. The horses were worn out and the whistling sound above their ears made them even more nervous.

Prosac again cracked his whip and this time caught Holmes on the hand. The detective cried out and passed the reins from one hand to the other. I could see that the hand was red and numb up to the bone.

We were now outside the city and with fewer obstacles in the way Holmes could hold the team of horses with one arm. Prosac cracked the whip a third time. It shivered near our heads, but this time Holmes succeeded in grabbing hold of it. He yanked it and it flew out of the fugitive's hand. It must have been painful for Holmes, although the cold may have numbed his sensitivity to pain. The detective gave me the reins and coiled up the whip.

"Keep her steady and don't let up!" he cried. "I will try to stop him!"

He braced his foot on the seat and leaned out of the wagon. He grabbed the whip in his left hand and cracked it twice overhead to warn the fleeing man. Prosac looked at us and tore like mad at the reins of his exhausted horse.

"Stop!" cried Holmes in vain.

Then he swung the whip and it whistled in the direction of Prosac. The tip flew close to his face, and as the impostor turned toward the sound, it slashed his lower lip. His face contorted in pain and blood trickled down his chin. He wiped it off with the back of his hand.

"You will pay for that, Holmes!" he cried. "But not today!"

"We're not parting company yet!" my friend replied. "Faster, Watson!"

"I can't get anything more out of them!" I said pointing to the horses who were foaming at the mouth. "Either we slow down or they will collapse!"

Holmes looked ahead and then at the whip in his hand.

"Try to get closer to the carriage!"

"For God's sake, Holmes!" I cried in horror. "You will kill yourself!"

"Do not fear, I can handle it! Hurry!"

I moved the wagon as close as possible to the side of the carriage without the wheels knocking each other, but the manoeuver cost us several yards. The coachbox of the wagon was now level with the back wheel of the carriage. Holmes, still holding onto the railing with one hand, snapped the whip and it wound around the handrail of Prosac's carriage. The detective pulled the whip taught and then leapt and swung in a graceful arc onto the carriage. He hung for a brief second above the road zooming beneath him and collided with the rear wall of the cab. Then he pulled himself up safely, using the luggage racks as handholds. He wanted to climb across the roof to the coachbox in front.

He clambered over the grate and kneeling looked around. He had to hold on with all his might, yet he pushed forward. My blood froze in my veins at the sight, but all I could do was keep as close as possible to the wildly careening carriage.

When Prosac saw him he dropped the reins and assumed a wide stance. I thought he had in mind to fight Holmes, but that was not the case. Quickly he pulled out the pin that kept the harness fastened to the carriage. Then he pushed off and leapt across the gap between the carriage and the horse. I must admit that it was marvellous.

There was nothing Holmes could now, because the road had become even bumpier and the carriage was bounding along like mad. He held on for dear life.

The fugitive's horse had begun to tire, but was still fresher than ours. Prosac mounted it bareback, twisted the reins tightly in one hand, leaned over the side at a perilous angle and undid the harness, swung back up again and repeated the daring procedure on the other side. The wooden shaft with its leather straps fell away and rolled on the ground.

Had I not seen it with my own eyes I would not have believed such a thing was possible outside the circus. Prosac's horse picked up speed and a moment later disappeared in the darkness.

It was no longer in our power to catch him. I had to focus now on Holmes, who remained trapped in the carriage, which was hurtling at headlong speed towards the trees on the shoulder of the road.

I yelled as loud as I could to warn him, but he was aware of the danger. Only seconds remained before the doomed carriage met its ruin. Holmes stood up on the roof and jumped. He flew into the grass on the shoulder, fell sharply and did several somersaults.

The carriage tilted over and smashed into the trees. I shuddered to think what would have happened had Holmes not jumped off.

I quickly guided the wagon toward the wreck and searched in the darkness for Holmes's body. I feared that he had broken his neck. The deadly stillness was a bad sign. I wished at least that I could hear moaning.

"I must admit that Monsieur Prosac surprised me with his acrobatic display," I suddenly heard behind me.

I looked around and saw a shadow rising off the ground. He was leaning on his arm with some difficulty, but was able to stand up.

"Holmes!" I cried with relief.

"I'm all right," he said, dusting off his jacket. "Just a little tired."

He shuffled to the wagon, clambered onto the seat and fainted dead away.

VII

Persona non grata

I drove the taciturn Holmes back to the city, where we first had to settle some unpleasant business. I stopped the wagon in front of the exalted entrance to the *Renaissance* Hotel, and to overcome the doorman's vociferous protestations, pressed a shilling into his palm.

"Take care of our carriage, boy!" I said.

Confused by the salutation, the old doorman ceased his objections, slid the coin into his pocket and with a bow took away the depleted geldings.

Holmes and I wearily climbed the stairs under the round marquise and entered the reception area, which was abuzz with excitement. The hotel restaurant was now empty except for a cleaning crew. As soon as the night receptionist noticed the detective's return he tried discretely to stop us.

"Gentlemen, would you be so kind and wait here a moment," the receptionist said to us and immediately called someone on the internal telephone. He also gave us a thick card of white paper on which there was a rather curt message from the Countess in which she asked us for an audience and explanation of the events at dinner.

She was not the only one who wanted an explanation. Running down the stairs was a little man with a waxed moustache, trembling with anger. It was the hotel manager.

"Are you Mr Holmes?" he asked.

"Yes," the detective said. "What can I do for you?"

The manager frowned and slammed his little fist repeatedly on the reception desk. Given his diminutive stature he had to stand up on tip toe to do so.

"You owe me an explanation, gentlemen! I must draw your attention to the fact that we expect a certain standard of behaviour from our guests! We are proud that our clients include many highly placed figures and members of noble families from all of Europe. We simply cannot afford such excesses!"

Holmes rubbed his bloodshot eyes and looked at the manager sadly. I wondered if his exhaustion would break his usual perfect reserve, but he kept calm.

"You must for the time being be satisfied merely with my apologies, sir. The rest will wait till morning. I am too tired to discuss the matter now. Goodnight."

And he turned around and headed up the staircase.

I fell asleep as soon as my head touched the pillow. I slept fully clothed and in my shoes, and yet it was one of the deepest sleeps of my life.

And also one of the shortest.

* * *

To make matters worse, Holmes's withdrawal paroxysms had returned with a vengeance. Perhaps it was due to exhaustion from the night's chase, but his body simply needed a crutch. In the middle of the night I was awoken by a banging from his room. I got up quickly, fearing for his health, and entered his room without knocking.

Holmes was in trousers and waistcoat; apparently he too had not bothered to get undressed. His room looked as though a battle had been fought in it. The drawers and cabinets were open and clothes were strewn everywhere. The detective stood in the midst of it all stood with a distant expression on his face.

"What's the meaning of this?" I cried.

He looked at my wildly, but said nothing. He continued rummaging through his suitcases frantically. Obviously he was looking for something and it was immediately clear what.

Cocaine.

His paroxysms were not as strong as they had been a few weeks ago, but when afflicted by them he was still oblivious to the world. In those moments he was completely dominated by a subconscious desire for the opiate and could be dangerous to himself and to others.

I returned to my room to fetch my medical bag. I quickly found a soothing preparation, which I had prudently prepared and packed with me, and when I returned to him he muttered something in confusion and pounded his fist into a cupboard. It was a miracle that he did not wake up the guests in the neighbouring rooms.

I leapt at him from behind and before he could stop me I injected the needle into a vein in his forearm. Fortunately it took effect almost immediately; otherwise he may have struck me. Holmes sank to the floor and lost consciousness. I dragged him back into bed and returned exhausted to my room.

* * *

I was roused from my slumber by a sharp rapping on the door. Slowly I returned to the world of reality. I turned in bed and looked out the window. It was damp and overcast. From the street below came the sounds of traffic, people shouting and carts clattering on the cobblestones.

The knocking became more insistent. The hands of the clock showed eight o'clock. Too early. But I got up and headed to the door, still in a daze. I expected to see the chambermaid, so I was all the more surprised to see two uniformed gendarmes standing in the hallway accompanied by the squirming hotel manager.

"Monsieur Holmes?" said one of them in accented English after clicking his heels together. "May we enter? We are from the police."

"No, he is still sleeping," I answered. "May I do something for you?"

The gendarmes looked crestfallen.

"It would be better to discuss it inside; we were asked not to cause any unnecessary commotion in the hallways," he said politely, but firmly, and without waiting for my consent entered the room. The manager nodded frantically, looking around the corridor.

Reluctantly I admitted them.

"I repeat that Mr Holmes is sleeping," I said, not wanting to explain to them why he was so exhausted. I could not tell them anything about his indisposition; admitting the detective's addiction would not achieve anything. "As soon as he is awake he will be happy to assist you with whatever you require."

"I suspect that there has been a misunderstanding," said one of the gendarmes. "We did not come for his help; we came to take him in for questioning!"

"Is he under arrest?"

"The chief used the term *bring him in*," said the gendarme. "Nevertheless, he was quite insistent. I am sorry, but you must come with us immediately."

"Did he say why?"

"I am not authorised to provide this information," he said. "May we speak with Mr Holmes?"

"I will see what I can do for you," I said.

I left our uninvited guests alone and knocked gently on the door of the other bedroom. As I expected nobody answered. I entered and in the gloom of the darkened windows spied Holmes's figure on the bed. He was sleeping on his stomach, dressed as I had left him, and was breathing peacefully. But I could not refuse the local police like I could in London. His name did not carry as much weight here.

I shook him by the shoulder.

"Yes?" he said quickly sitting up. "Are they here yet?"

"Who?" I asked, taken aback by the speed with which he awoke. I had to admire his alacrity. He never wasted time with morning drowsiness. He was always able to arise immediately and function at the highest level.

"The police, of course. Who else?"

"How did you know?"

74

"We have a lot of explaining to do," he said. "Indeed, today we will probably do little else. Tell them that I will be with them directly."

Then he passed his hand over his unshaven chin and corrected himself.

"Actually, tell them fifteen minutes. And you put yourself together too, Watson. Today we will face the wrath of the *Gendarmerie* together!"

"How otherwise," I nodded.

The officers accepted my assurances and agreed to wait downstairs in the lobby.

After a short drive we stopped in front of a tall white building with a gleaming brass plate on clean plaster. It was the *Préfecture de Police*, the main headquarters of the Paris police. We were politely escorted to the upper floor, where the gendarmes bade us sit in a tastefully furnished drawing room. I understood that an audience with the chief of police himself awaited us.

Holmes regarded the upholstered sofa with the same expression that he would have the barred cell of the most gruesome prison. We stared at the door, though which a junior officer disappeared carrying a file.

"What are they going to do with us?" I asked.

"They will no doubt ask us a fantastic number of questions about the events of yesterday evening," he said. "Get ready, it will be quite arduous."

"Will we face charges?"

"I am not certain whether an apology will suffice. The chief of police is known for his love of tidiness. He certainly cannot be pleased with what transpired last night."

"But they cannot punish us!" I cried. "He owes you at least that much!"

"I expect that we shall not be prosecuted. In any case, the responsibility is mine. You, Watson, were just an innocent victim of my zeal."

"Even you don't believe that!"

"I insist on it. Were it not for my vanity, none of this would have happened. I had not expected Prosac to put up such a resistance."

He took off his coat and threw it over the back of the chair. No doubt he would have loved to smoke, but there was nothing in the room to light his pipe with. He chewed nervously on the stem of his pipe and drummed his fingers on the arm of the chair.

"How did it start anyway?"I asked after a short while. "One moment we were dining peacefully and the next we were racing through the night on a wagon!"

"Prosac surprised me," he admitted. "I followed him into the bathroom with the intention of ending that disgusting charade. I wanted to convince him to part with the Countess in a considerate manner that would not cause suspicion and then take him away. When I entered the bathroom he was waiting for me behind the door. He hit me over the head with something and for a brief moment I lost consciousness."

He touched the top of his head.

"You know the rest," he continued. "As soon as I regained consciousness I ran after him."

"Quite a violent reaction for a con artist!"

"I would not be surprised if we discover that Mr Prosac is much more than just a con artist. So far we have only seen the tip of the iceberg."

I did not get a chance to learn more, because an official nodded to us that we could now enter the office. The chief of police sat at a long mahogany desk with the contents of a large file spread out before him. His high-backed chair was turned towards the window, through which the Eiffel Tower could be seen glittering in the distance. When the door clicked shut behind us he turned around to look at us.

Alphonse Bertillon* had that year celebrated his fiftieth birthday, but he looked older, the result of greying sideburns, tired eyes and a lifetime of hard work. The success of the methods that he had originated had brought him to the very top of the police force, even though they would not prove to be long lasting. He turned toward us and placed the file on the desk.

"I did not expect our next meeting to occur under such circumstances, Holmes," he said reproachfully, gazing at the detective over the top of his glasses. "If I'm not mistaken you are usually on our side of the law."

"I am always in the service of justice."

"Indeed?"

Bertillon briefly looked into some papers and began to read aloud.

"Disturbing the peace, assaulting restaurant staff, theft of a wagon, impersonating a police officer, reckless endangerment... Should I continue?"

"That will not be necessary."

"I agree," he said. "I expect some kind of explanation from you."

We sat down and my friend briefly summarised the reason for our trip to Paris and everything that had led up to the night's events. He also described the chase, but failed to mention that he had nearly lost his life on the roof of the carriage. He concluded with a report on the current condition of the geldings and the wagon and expressed his gratitude and apologies as well as his intention to repay the rightful owner. The chief heard him out attentively.

"Paris is not London, my friend," he said when Holmes had finished.

He glanced at the portrait of President Loubet on the wall. The bitterness in his voice had disappeared.

"We haven't seen such goings on here in a long time," he said.

"It was not –"

"I know, I know," said Bertillon. "You know what I mean."

77

He stood up and looked out the window.

"As noble as your intentions are, I cannot accept wild chases through the streets in stolen vehicles. That poor country fellow in our department in Rue Trafalgar –"

The clanging of the telephone unexpectedly disturbed us and turned the chief's attention away. He listened to the receiver with increasing amazement.

"Cabbage? Dammit, what cabbage?"

I looked with horror at Holmes, fearing that our bill would rise even more, but he did not seem in the least disturbed, and just winked at me.

"Heads of cabbage?" Bertillon cried into the telephone. "Are you drunk, man? Immediately report to the chief of your department! I will have you checked!"

He slammed down the receiver and scribbled a note on a piece of paper.

"Can you believe it? This fellow must be drunk on duty! Apparently he has received numerous reports of large amounts of cabbage being found in flower beds!"

"That would never happen in England," said Holmes.

The director scowled and returned to what he had been saying.

"With regard to your previous service to the French police I am willing to turn a blind eye on your transgressions."

He got up from the desk with the list of offences, crumpled it and tossed it in the waste bin.

"De facto, the case is closed."

"Dr Watson and I are grateful."

"Nevertheless," he continued, "I assume that nothing of the sort will happen again! The next time you follow a suspect in our country, please inform me in advance. None of this would have happened yesterday had you requested the assistance of the *gendarmerie*!"

"I shall try to comply."

"In your shoes I would focus on the word *comply*!" said Bertillon, returning to his chair. "And now let us not take up any more of each other's time."

We got up to leave.

"Just one more thing!" Bertillon added. "Can you tell me when you plan to leave?"

Holmes stood up straight and looked thoughtful.

"With Prosac's escape the situation has become somewhat more complex. We do not have very many clues and will probably have to remain in Paris for a few more weeks. I will, however, restrain myself in my methods, sir."

Bertillon looked dispirited.

"May my men be of any assistance in speeding up this process?"

"There may be a certain record in the archive of the Sûreté that would help us embark on the next phase of the investigation as soon as tomorrow. In all likelihood our suspect has already left your jurisdiction."

"Just as *you* will, I hope," said the chief.

He called to his assistant.

"Very well, Holmes, but you must find the document yourself. I don't have enough men to play these games with you."

"Sir?" said the assistant who had just entered.

"Take the gentlemen to the archive," Bertillon ordered. "They may examine any records they wish, with the exception of those marked top secret."

"We will not need them," said Holmes. "I know them, anyway. After all, I helped compile them."

"Be done by evening!" said Bertillon peevishly.

He shook our hands and then closed the thick file on the desk.

"That's settled then," he said giving it to the assistant, and he quickly got to work on something else.

The assistant escorted us out of the office and closed the door behind us.

"Well, that wasn't so bad" I said with relief.

"No, the hard work is ahead of us," replied the detective.

"You mean the archive?"

"We will spend all day underground in a damp and dusty room, squinting at tiny letters under bad light. We will not be able to rest until we find something."

"But that's not even the worst of it," he added. "We then have to face the Countess!"

---

*   Adolphe Bertillon (1853–1914) – French criminal investigator, founder of bertillonage.

VIII

Hope Dies Last

Holmes was right about the conditions in the archive. We were led to a foul-smelling windowless basement, lit only by a weak electric light, entirely insufficient for the size of the room. Tall shelves full of files lined the walls on every side.

A hunched archivist reluctantly showed us to a table, dumped a pile of files on it and scuttled away. I blew a layer of dust from the uppermost file and coughed.

"Is this truly necessary?"I asked unhappily.

"It is regrettable," replied Holmes, who was already perusing the files."But do not despair, my friend. The condition of the files is better than I expected!"

I looked at the file on the table marked with a numerical cipher and opened it. Inside were five yellowing papers covered in faded ink and a stiff card.

"Are you certain about this?" I said. "You expect to find something of use here?"

"Certainly!"

He spread the papers over the table and turned over the stiff card. It was only then that I noticed it was a photograph.

"Bertillon instituted a system of photographic identification. An arrested person is photographed from three sides: from the front and from each profile!"

"How simple and effective!"

"A trait common to all brilliant ideas," he said. "And now let us get to work. I tried to make our investigation as simple as possible. As you can see, none of these records is less than five years old. They cannot be more recent, because Prosac was already in England. From here we will continue into the past!"

"What if we go through all of them without unearthing anything?"

"That will not happen," said the detective confidently and he plunged into his work.

He was now completely detached from the outside world and it was useless to try and talk to him. So I too went to work, dreary as it was.

Hours passed. Holmes and I went through an endless series of files, one by one. He surely would have liked to smoke, but it was strictly prohibited in the archive. For my part I would have been happy to get something to eat, but I did not dare suggest a break. My back ached from bending over the table, my fingers were as dry as paper and my mouth burned with dust. I assumed that Holmes felt the same way, but he continued to leaf through the files, like some kind of tremendous machine.

Just when I had started to fear that it would never end the detective sat up straight.

"Eureka!" he cried.

"You found it?"

"Yes, in all likelihood," he said squinting at the photograph. "He is thinner and has a beard, but without a doubt it is our man!"

"May I see?"

Holmes wordlessly handed me the photograph.

It did not look much like Prosac to me. Had the photograph ended up in my hands first I would certainly have passed it over without a second glance. I told Holmes as much.

"In that case we are most fortunate that I found it!"he said. "Look more closely."

Upon closer inspection I had to admit a certain resemblance, and the longer I looked at the likeness, the more clearly I recognised Prosac's features. It required a little imagination, something that Holmes often reproached me for lacking.

"My God," I said. "It is him! How did you recognise him so quickly?"

"Practice," he said, shrugging. "People in my line of work learn to see things differently than others. We do not focus on the whole but on certain specific parts. As a doctor you must know that the face and thus a person's whole appearance can very easily be altered. A beard, hair, a scar; all these things can change a face immensely! And that's not to mention intentional changes, when the face is surgically altered to give the person a completely different appearance. Fortunately, this method is prohibitively expensive and therefore exceedingly rare."

"In any case," he continued, "certain features can be modified only with great difficulty or not at all, hence these are the best suited for criminological identification. The hairline, the shape of the ear and the placement of the eyes, these are always the first things that I look at."

"You are right," I said examining the photograph.

Prosac's greasy hair stuck in clumps to the sides of his head and the thin haggard face exuded a kind of animal aggression. Perhaps this was what made him so attractive to the fairer sex, especially when he was washed, shaven and elegantly dressed.

Holmes pushed aside the other files, leaving only Prosac's file in front of us. It was surprisingly slim.

"Let us see what led our friend astray," said the detective."His real name is Michal Kuzmic. He's from somewhere in Central Europe. So far we have only known him by his aliases."

In my mind I now assigned the fourth name to the same face.

"It's no surprise that he ended up where he is now," said Holmes, leafing through the file. "He grew up on the streets of Vienna, with no family, and in the company of loose women. He ran away from a gang of Tatar marauders who wanted to sell him to the circus. This fits in with everything that we know about him so far. And based on his superior riding skills, which we witnessed yesterday, it is possible that you were right about the injury to young St. John-Smythe. And the courtesans that Kuzmic grew up with probably taught him how to play on the emotions of women, a talent that he has employed to brilliant effect! He ran afoul of the law from an early age, but they were only minor offences, pick pocketing and small confidence schemes. Nothing terrible when you consider the conditions in which he grew up. His first conviction was at the age of twenty. He got six months for jewellery theft."

"A pretty big step up from a small-time thief!"

"That was in October 1894,"said Holmes. "Since then he has been on his best behaviour."

"Or they didn't catch him for anything."

"That seems more likely. Aha, this is interesting!"he cried. "This record says that he was part of the gang of our notorious friend Rudolf Mayer, who at that time was already a major player in the local criminal underground!"

"The gang probably helped keep his record clean," I said.

"Yes, but two years later this changed," he said, reading onwards. "Aha, so that is why our efforts met with such dogged defiance! That is why he left France!"

"Do not keep me in suspense! Why?"

The detective quickly scanned the lines.

"Do you remember that post office robbery in Lyon in the spring of ninety-seven in which several tens of thousands of pounds was lost?"

"Yes, I remember, they wrote about it in the English papers. A guard was killed in the robbery."

"The police immediately caught all the robbers, except for one," Holmes continued. "The other robbers blamed him for the murder. They ended up in jail, but the money was never found. Some of them are free again."

"I still don't understand what this has to do with our case..."

The detective handed me the file.

"According to this the murderer and the missing robber was Kuzmic. It is also clear that the money ended up with him!"

"So we are dealing with a murderer?"

"My friend, you are simplicity itself," he sighed. "In fact the murderer was in all likelihood somebody else, even though today we obviously cannot prove it!"

"I've probably lost the thread somewhere," I said. "I do not understand what you are telling me!"

"It is as clear as day that Kuzmic was a sacrificial lamb! He was never a violent person. As he managed to escape they blamed everything on him. I presume that he was well paid for this. Our friend left France and began a new life in England."

"And then?"

"From then I can only make deductions," he conceded. "Perhaps he spent all the money on a life of excess or he missed the thrill of crime and embarked on a career as a con artist. His old contacts got him all the way to Thorpe. Now he has returned and thanks to me he must again flee. When I catch him they will put him on trial for the murder of that policeman."

"But that would cost him his head!"

"I know," he said. "But his crimes are not negligible."

"What shall we do?"

"We'll address that when he have captured him," said the detective.

He closed the file and called over the archivist.

"We are leaving. Please ensure that this message is delivered directly to the hands of Mr Bertillon."

He handed the man a folded piece of paper on which he had hastily scribbled a few sentences.

"And give him my warm regards!"

We left the building and I inhaled with relief the fresh air outside. It was three o'clock and high time for lunch. We flagged the first carriage that we saw.

"May I ask what you wrote in your message?" I asked curiously as our carriage trundled along. "Did you tell him that we found a link to that old robbery?"

"No, I kept that for myself, until I learn the background of the whole tangled story. I only told Bertillon that we were leaving. He will no doubt be pleased."

"Are we going to Vienna? After Mayer?"

"After Mayer yes, but not to Vienna. I am told that he is now in Bohemia, in Prague to be precise."

He pronounced the name of this city sombrely, as he always did whenever he mentioned this part of Austria-Hungary. It reminded him of that long-ago case that ended in defeat*and which had returned to his thoughts in these troubled months following the death of Irene Adler.

"In Vienna the police are already hot on his heels, which is why he decided to move his operation. Prague is ideal. It is large enough, international, and the right distance from Vienna."

"And how will we..."

"We can converse with the locals in German," said Holmes, anticipating my question.

We spent the rest of the trip in silence. The detective looked increasingly gloomy and walked the last few steps to the hotel at a glacial pace. I suspected why. A pile of messages from the Countess awaited us at the reception desk.

It was hard to believe that he was the same man who had calmly marched to a duel with Professor Moriarty, who had not flinched in the face of mortal danger, a man before whom the London underworld trembled.

He knocked on the Countess's door, probably hoping that no one would answer. To his misfortune the door opened and there, like the goddess of vengeance, stood the Countess d'Ambolieu.

"Enter, gentlemen," she said quietly. "We have much to discuss."

I will not describe our whole conversation. Suffice to say that it was not easy and did not reveal anything that the attentive reader does not already knew. The Countess learned the truth about her fiancé or at least as much of it as Holmes chose to tell her. He refrained from revealing certain details that would make the situation even more difficult for her, such as the full story of young St. John-Smythe or what we had found in the archives of the Sûreté. Then she coolly bade us adieu, and we went to our rooms where we packed for the journey.

I regretted that we would no longer enjoy the company of this vivacious woman and that we had parted ways so bitterly. She had shed no tears, but her pride clearly was wounded.

By dinnertime we were seated in the compartment of a train bound for Prague. The whistle blew and we slowly drove out of Paris. All that I had seen of this marvellous city were the streets during the night chase and the underground archive.

I leaned back in my seat across from Holmes and unfolded a copy of the *Times*. But before I could really dip into it someone else entered the compartment.

"You didn't think you could leave without me, gentlemen!" chirped the Countess, whose voice no longer bore any traces of bitterness. "May I join you?"

"Countess!" said Holmes in surprise.

"Kuzmic picked the wrong woman to trick. He will find out what it's like to be a hunted animal! The game is afoot!"

With these fiery words she took a seat and remained with us for the rest of the journey.

We arrived in Prague late at night. The station platform was empty, save for a stout gentleman in a bowler hat sitting on a bench. The platform was shrouded in clouds of steam as we disembarked from the train.

"Do you know a good hotel here?" the Countess asked, looking with suspicion at the man on the bench, who was heading towards us. "What does he want?"

I wondered the same.

The gentleman was barrel-shaped with a round face dominated by an enormous moustache. He held a greasy package containing some sort of food that he munched as he walked. As he neared us he put the package in his breast pocket, wiped his mouth and cleaned his hand on his vest.

"I was beginning to think you'd never arrive," he said in fluent, though somewhat odd German, and held out his hand. "I am Inspector Ledvina. Our police chief received word that you were on your way here. I have been asked to ensure that you do not cause an uproar similar to the one yesterday in Paris. With all due respect, of course."

"I see," said Holmes with distaste. "This will be Bertillon's doing."

"Indeed," said Ledvina. "And I was so looking forward to a bit of excitement."

The detective turned to him and winked good-naturedly.

"Hope dies last, inspector!"

---

* See *A Scandal in Bohemia.*

IX

Mimicry

In addition to sending the chubby inspector to meet us at the station, the Prague chief of police had kindly arranged accommodation for us at the Adria Hotel. An hour after arriving at the station our heads were already nestled in the hotel's soap-scented pillows.

I was grateful for this small kindness and believed that Holmes secretly was too. His increasingly poorly concealed annoyance and the paroxysm that had afflicted him the night before in Paris were warnings that everything was still far from all right with him.

But a peaceful eight-hour sleep visibly restored to him a measure of strength. That morning at breakfast Holmes appeared completely normal, and my only concern was the return of his occasional lack of appetite. We were soon joined in the dining room by the Countess. I did not want to discuss Holmes's health in front of her, and so I had to satisfy myself with mere observation.

"Where shall we begin our investigation?" the Countess asked as soon as she had taken her seat.

Evidently her vengeful spirits of the day before and her resolve to hunt down her former fiancé were as strong as ever.

Holmes stopped sipping his tea and looked at her with gentle amusement.

"You waste no time!"

"At my age I can't afford to," she joked, pouring herself a cup of coffee. "I must dispose of one man before I can pursue another."

"Paris must be full of men who would be happy to oblige."

"True," said the Countess drily. "Except that half of them look like your prime minister. No, the choice is not easy."

Holmes passed over the slight to Mr Balfour*. I for my part continued with my breakfast, which was a pleasant change to what we usually have in Britain. The bread in particular was delectable. On the other hand, the coffee was horrid and the tea weak and without milk.

"The investigation must begin with a reconnaissance of the terrain," said Holmes after we had eaten. "I propose that we spend the day touring the city."

"Is that not pointless?" said the Countess.

"Not at all, my dear," said the detective. "Thorough familiarity with the environment in which our investigation will be conducted is a basic key to success. We must blend into the surroundings so that our enemy does not notice the net being cast around him. Only then will we have a chance to succeed."

"In that case let us meet in the lobby in twenty minutes," said the Countess.

As soon as she had run off to get changed I leaned over to Holmes. I wanted to determine whether he was indeed feeling better than the night before, but he dismissed me brusquely.

"Don't be a nanny, Watson," he retorted irritably.

I was ready to be offended, but then his voice softened.

"Of course I appreciate your concern. But I want to forget my problems and you keep trying to remind me of them."

His behaviour surprised me, but I decided not to quarrel with him. Perhaps he was right and he only needed a distraction. A walk through the city seemed ideal for this purpose. It was another clear day and Prague enticed us out for a sightseeing tour of its ancient monuments.

Holmes and I went to our rooms to fetch our overcoats. We had planned to meet in the hallway, but Holmes did not appear. Something had apparently delayed him. I knocked on the door of his room and found Holmes at the window, watching the street from behind the curtain.

"Is something happening?"

"Nothing that I have not expected," he sighed and motioned to me to look.

I did not see anything out of the ordinary.

"Watson, you can be so blind," he sighed. "Look closely at the other side of the street, in the shadow of the lamp."

Indeed, leaning nonchalantly on the lamppost in an inconspicuous bowler was Inspector Ledvina, watching the door to our hotel.

Clearly he had been ordered to keep a close eye on us.

"What shall we do with him?"

"What can we do?" said Holmes, shrugging indifferently. "We shall leave that up to him."

"Shall we leave by the back door?"

"No, there is no reason. Let's let the inspector follow us. I don't plan to do anything today that would be cause for concern."

We met the Countess in the lobby and together left the hotel, which was right on the city's main boulevard, Wenceslas Square. As soon as Ledvina saw us, he pulled his bowler lower over his forehead and made ready to follow us.

Holmes went straight to him and greeted him loudly. This caught the inspector completely off guard.

"Where are you off to, friends?"he asked as we approached. "A walk?"

"It would be a sin to stay indoors on a day such as this."

"Indeed," said Ledvina. "Well, I happened to be in the neighbourhood, so I said to myself that I'd stop by."

"Nonsense, you are just following us!" said the Countess

The genial policemen looked crestfallen. The thankless task that he had been assigned was obviously not one he relished.

"Not at all, my dear inspector; in fact you are just the man we need," said Holmes. "We very much need a guide to Prague!"

Ledvina brightened and smoothed his moustache with his fingers.

"Glad to be of service, Mr Holmes. And what would you like to see of our fair city?"

Holmes looked around.

Our hotel was at the epicentre of the city's social and political life. The wide, oblong square with an electric railway running down the middle sloped gently upwards, culminating in a grand neo-Renaissance building.

The inspector noticed us gazing at it and his eyes brightened.

"That is our new national museum," he said proudly.

Clearly the building was of great significance to the Czechs, who for years had suffered under the yoke of the mighty Austro-Hungarian Empire.

"The construction was completed just a couple of years ago," Ledvina said eagerly.

"It is beautiful," I said.

"It contains many unique collections," Ledvina continued. "In addition to mineralogical–"

"But we shan't spend the day chattering on the streets, shall we?" the Countess interjected. "The museum is no doubt beautiful, but that can wait. Let us go already!"

Ledvina's eyes shone.

"Am I keeping you from something?"

The inspector's appearance was kind and sincere, but no doubt a keen mind was at work beneath his bowler hat, studying our every word. It would not help our cause to reveal to him the true purpose of our visit.

"Certainly not," said Holmes. "The Countess d'Ambolieu probably just does not want to stand outside in the cold."

"Oh, I know somewhere cosy and warm," said the inspector smiling. "Why didn't you say so in the first place? Follow me!"

Prague is a city of many wonders, but according to Inspector Ledvina the most wondrous of these is the *U Primasù* pub.

I certainly had no objections.

We spent most of the day conversing over pints of foamy amber ale in the pub. In the afternoon we finally bade farewell to Ledvina, mainly because the Countess was growing increasingly impatient, and headed back to the hotel.

"Gentlemen, you have disappointed me," the Countess said as we trundled along in the tram, which we had decided to try for the return journey to the hotel. The vehicle rocked back and forth, which in combination with the beer gave me an irresistible urge to sleep.

"I imagined our little excursion somewhat differently," she continued.

Holmes, as usual, was immune to the insidious effects of alcohol.

"Watson and I will make it up to you," he said with a smile. "I am sorry that you had to stay with us so late today, but at least we have appeased our friend from the police. Now he will no doubt give us several hours to gain strength."

"I do not understand how such a person can hold a position in the police force."

The Countess was alluding to the fact that Ledvina was by all appearances a regular customer in the pub. The staff greeted him by name, as did many dubious-looking women, whom Ledvina shamelessly flattered and pinched.

"I dare say that I admire the inspector," said Holmes.

"Excuse me?"

"These convivial contacts with the underworld can be very beneficial. People often let slip seemingly inconsequential information in these environments and the inspector is capitalising on this aspect of human nature."

"Except that it can also work the other way," said the Countess.

"Indeed, but I do not think this is the case. Did you notice that Ledvina was sober the whole time we were in the pub? The man knows how to hold his liquor."

"So do we," I hiccupped.

"Naturally, Watson. But there is another reason, Madame, why I consider this alcoholic interlude as having been beneficial to our cause."

"Pray tell. Had I wanted to spend the day drinking I could have stayed in Paris!"

"While you and Watson were reflecting on door-to-door salesmen and cigarette sellers, Ledvina and I discussed many important things. As a colleague the inspector wanted to impress me with his success and so I managed to extract a lot of useful information from him. A veritable gold mine!"

"Tell us!"

"Through seemingly unrelated scraps Ledvina provided me with details about the local underworld and the manner of its organisation. Had I asked him directly, I would not have learned half of what I did by letting him talk freely."

"In that case..."

"In that case, we can thank the inspector's zeal," said Holmes. "In one afternoon of drinking at the pub I have managed to gather more information than I would have over several days in the field. Tomorrow therefore we can focus on sightseeing."

"It seems that I owe you another apology, Mr Holmes."

"Nonsense," he said, waving his hand.

The tram rumbled to a stop in front of our hotel.

We each went to our rooms and I used the next few hours for a refreshing nap. When I awoke it was already dark outside. I might have been willing to forgo dinner, turn on my side and sleep some more, but I suddenly heard a strange clatter in Holmes's room.

Immediately I remembered his last withdrawal paroxysm. Anticipating the worst I grabbed an injection and ran to his room.

I was ready for anything. Or so I thought.

I yanked open the door, but instead of Holmes standing in the middle of the room was a tall man in a brown leather coat and cap. He glared at me from behind bushy brows and his left cheek twitched.

At first I thought that a burglar had broken into Holmes's room.

I wanted to yell for help, but the lummox guessed my intentions and threw a pillow at me.

Before I could fend off the projectile he lunged at me and twisted my arm behind my back. In that fraction of a second I did not even notice that he did this with a strange gentleness, as though he were trying not to hurt me.

"Quiet, Watson," he commanded and forced me to sit on the couch.

I only realised that he had addressed me by name when he stood up and removed some wadding from his cheeks which deformed his face and forced him to mumble. When he pulled off his eyebrows I felt as though struck by lightning.

"I must learn to get used to your disguises, Holmes," I said humiliated.

"There is no higher complement," said the detective, rubbing his temples wearily. "If I can fool you, who knows me better than anyone in the world, then I can fool anybody."

I did not want to leave him alone in this state, so I offered to accompany him.

"Should I get dressed too?"

"Thank you, but not this time, my friend. My head hurts a little, but some fresh air will help. Now, however, I must head out on my own and as inconspicuously as possible. Hence I have disguised myself as a local coachman."

I was overcome with curiosity.

"Where are you going?"

"So far fortune has favoured us, but now we must grab it by the horns. Ledvina mentioned a place called the Poison Shack. It is where the Prague criminal element gathers at night to gamble and deal drugs. An interesting excursion no doubt. With a little bit of luck I will discover where Kuzmic is hiding out."

Holmes turned off the light and looked out the window.

"The wolf again lurks beneath the window," he said, pointing at Inspector Ledvina who was back at his post beneath the street lamp. "I will need you to do something for me, Watson."

"Certainly."

"Go down to the restaurant for dinner and take the Countess with you. Announce loudly that I am in my room resting. The wait staff will certainly relay the message to Ledvina and so he will suspect nothing."

"Agreed!"

The detective again donned his false eyebrows, returned the wadding to his mouth and hunched forward slightly.

"It's time to go," he said. "*Bonne appétit!*"

Then this strange creature into which Holmes had transformed himself bounded out the door and disappeared around the corner of the hallway.

It seemed to be another of the detective's ingenious plans.

* Arthur James Balfour (1848–1930) was the English prime minister from 1902–1905.

X

Golem's Shadow

I waited for Holmes long into the night. Around three in the morning not even coffee could keep me awake and I was so overcome with fatigue that I put aside my book and went to bed.

He must have returned sometime in the early morning. Half asleep I heard the doors bang and Holmes walking about the room. Soothed by these sounds I turned over on my other side. I could wait to learn about the course of the mission tomorrow at breakfast.

But that morning at the table Holmes was again strangely agitated and close-lipped. He reeked of smoke, ate almost nothing, and was out of sorts. The night's excursion had clearly exhausted him and returned him to the condition that preceded a paroxysm. I therefore recommended that he spend the morning resting, prepared the necessary medicines should the worst happen, and hoped that I was just being overanxious.

Today even the Countess sensed that Holmes was not entirely well. Soon after breakfast she ventured out into the city alone saying that she intended to visit several fashion houses.

I spent the morning in my room. I wanted to use the time to take care of my correspondence. I needed to reply to a letter from my assistant who was seeking advice regarding a certain thorny medical question.

But the flow of my thoughts was interrupted several minutes later by a commotion beneath my window. It was hopeless to try to ignore it, so I got up to see what the fuss was about.

On the street a newsvendor was hawking the latest edition. Customers flocked around him like pigeons.

Something important must have happened.

I ran downstairs and managed to buy the very last copy.

The headline was shocking:

Golem Kills in Jewish Cemetery!

PRAGUE – The body of a strangled young woman was found in the Old Jewish Cemetery last night. The police are withholding details of the case as the investigation is ongoing. Our paper, however, has spoken to a woman who says she witnessed the murder. She describes the killer as a giant monster with glowing eyes. The body was discovered near the grave of Rabbi Loew, and the Jews are saying it is the work of their legendary protector, the Golem. The Prague police have no comment.

I had barely finished reading the article when a window opened above me and Holmes's dishevelled head emerged.

"Watson!" he cried. "What is this clamour that prevents me from sleeping?"

"A murder!" I said, holding up the paper.

The word was like an elixir. His face, which this morning had resembled a heap of ashes, brightened with interest.

"Really? In that case please bring me a copy!"

When I entered his room he ripped the paper out of my hands impatiently.

"Fascinating," he said, tossing the paper into the corner as he did back home in Baker Street. "Let us go look at the scene of the crime, Watson!"

"That's not a good idea. The police might think that we want to interfere with their work."

"We shall not interfere in the least. We shall just take a look around."

"Shouldn't we focus on our case?"

"I have not forgotten. Last night in the Poison Shack I succeeded in penetrating the network, but until our adversary makes a wrong move there is nothing we can do but wait. And you well know that in my case idle hands are the devil's workshop."

Against this I had no argument.

* * *

When Holmes and I passed under the gate of the Old Jewish Cemetery I was overpowered by a strange feeling of anxiety. Even for a rationally minded person like me this place felt confining and frightening.

The relatively small cemetery, surrounded by an ancient brick wall, contained several hundred disordered tombstones, most of them neglected and overgrown with grass and weeds.

"Prague's Jews lived under the threat of senseless massacres throughout the Middle Ages," said Holmes as we walked in a remote part of the cemetery. "As elsewhere in the world they had to stick to get her just to survive."

By now we had reached an ancient tomb near the wall, where two policemen were shuffling about. The dead body still lay at the scene of the crime.

It was an ugly scene.

The upper half of the dead woman's body was lying on a shabby tombstone, with the head tilted up at an angle. The cause of death was clear. The eyes bulged and a swollen, purple tongue protruded from the bitten and bloody lips. Her clothes were simple and dirty, but not torn. Judging from the gaudy make-up hidden under the bruises of her face the dead woman had in all likelihood made a living selling her body.

"We are fortunate," cried Holmes.

His joyous exclamation so surprised the policemen that it took them a few moments to realise what was happening and tell Holmes to back away. Fortunately, as the coroner was finished with his examination of the body, the detective was free to have a look around.

"Local interest has been aroused by nothing more than the most primitive murder in the heat of passion," he said after a moment.

"Is it not rather the horrific place in which it took place?"

"That is true," said Holmes, examining the epitaph on the tombstone of Rabbi Judah Loew ben Bezalel, who had died in 1609. While the name of this Prague rabbi meant nothing to me, the detective regarded the tombstone with great interest.

"Who was he, Holmes? And who is this mysterious Golem that they are talking about? Was he a monster, a freak of nature?"

"According to legend, Rabbi Loew fashioned a human-like giant out of clay, which he brought to life with a magic Hebrew incantation to protect the Jews of Prague from their oppressors."

"And what happened to him? I mean according to legend?"

"I don't know," said Holmes. "I only remember that he defied his master and was destroyed. But I doubt very much that he would come to life after centuries and murder a woman in the cemetery."

The corpse fixed us with its motionless gaze, as though in supplication to the great Sherlock Holmes that he identify and convict her killer.

"Do you think she was raped?"

This question caught Holmes off guard.

"That is rather a question for a doctor."

"Should I examine her?"

"No, I do not think that is necessary. Nothing suggests it. Although she appears to have been a prostitute, it does not look as though the murder was motivated by lust."

"What then?"

Holmes frowned.

"Perhaps if they let me examine the body more thoroughly... At first glance, however, I would probably eliminate robbery too."

He suddenly frowned and stooped to inspect the dead woman's hands.

"But I may have rushed to judgment. Do you see the bruised skin on the ring finger of the left hand? There was a ring there recently!"

"Could it have fallen off while she struggled with the killer?"

"Rings don't just fall off. Judging by the mark on the finger it was quite tight."

He began studying her face carefully.

"Have you found something?"

"A number of bruises and lacerations. In addition to her neck there is bruising on the hands and feet."

"That is to be expected considering how she died."

"But some of the bruises are obviously much older. Look, these are almost invisible; this one is fresh and here you see a small scar that is already almost healed."

I knelt at the edge of the tomb in order to see where Holmes was pointing and I had to admit that his medical conclusions were faultless.

"Nevertheless, I don't see anything suspicious in it," I said, shrugging. "The girl made her living on the street. And perhaps she had a husband or a lover who beat her."

"Yes, no doubt she was often beaten."

"By her killer?"

"We must wait until we have more information before making accusations. In any case I would like to meet this person. At the very least he could describe the lost ring. And this could be the perfect clue to lead us to the murderer."

As though he had concluded that there was nothing more to be gleaned from the pale, listless face of the dead woman, who under other circumstances perhaps may even have been beautiful, Holmes stood up quickly and under the suspicious gaze of the policemen again began searching the area.

"The footprints are already destroyed," he grumbled. "Hopefully my Czech colleagues examined them before so thoroughly scattering them about."

"Did she die here or did the killer pull the body over from somewhere else?"

"The murder definitely took place here," said Holmes. "Besides, the newspaper said there was a witness. Until she speaks our speculations will be of little import."

"Will they let us talk with her?"

"Why would they do that Watson?" he exclaimed. "Don't forget that we are not at home in London where the police seek out my help. I am afraid that here, as you yourself correctly stated, they would see it as an interference in their internal affairs, especially after our notorious Parisian escapade."

"What a pity. I don't want to just wait for Prosac, or whatever his name is, to finally crop up."

"Neither do I," said Holmes sadly. "Unfortunately we have no other choice. Perhaps it is best that way."

A crew carrying a simple wooden coffin now entered the cemetery. It was time for us to leave.

Meanwhile a small demonstration had gathered outside.

At the synagogue neighbouring the cemetery there were nearly a hundred agitated people. Based on the yarmulkes on the heads of the men I concluded that most of them were Jewish, inhabitants of this cramped and unhygienic quarter of the city. The poverty of their clothes was in stark contrast to the well-kept synagogue with its brick gable, outbuildings and finely carved portal.

"*Beth Chaim, Beth Chaim,*" the angry assembly murmured.

On the steps in front of the entrance a bearded rabbi stood on a crate. He wore a black robe and a wide-brimmed hat, from beneath which hung long ringlets. He addressed the crows and waved a copy of today's paper in his hands.

"What is *Beth Chaim*?" I asked

"It means house of life," he said. "It is a reference to the cemetery. Apparently they fear its desecration, hence the assembly."

We came closer in order to hear what the rabbi would say. Fortunately he spoke in German and I was able to understand most of it.

"Friends, brothers!" he cried. "The time of our liberation is at hand!"

The crowd murmured.

"We can no longer tolerate the attacks of those who consider us inferior!"

A man in front of me raised a clenched fist and shouted something in Yiddish, which I did not understand.

"The Golem has finally returned to protect us! We no longer need be afraid! One glance sears our enemies and crushes them into the dust!"

"Is it true?" someone in the crowd cried. "Have you seen him?"

The rabbi raised his hand for silence.

"Sister Sara, who is here with us, witnessed his return last night!"

The rabbi motioned to an austere-looking woman with untidy hair to join him. She began to tell her version of the night's events, but her dramatic gesticulations and recitation only made Holmes smile. He found her description of the Golem especially amusing. She described it as a hybrid spawn of hell and a son of god.

When the woman finished her story a hush fell over the crowd. At that moment nobody doubted that the Golem, just as Moses had led the Jews out of Egypt, would now lead the citizens of the Prague ghetto across the sea of hatred to the Promised Land.

But then Holmes called out in his harsh German.

"With all due respect, what role did the dead woman play in all of this? Why did the Golem kill her?"

The crowd turned to look at him and then turned again to the rabbi.

"We all know how she made her living," said Sara. "Who among us has she not seduced with her evil ways? The ruin of many families is on her conscience! She was dirt which had to be flushed out!"

This outpouring of hatred caught Holmes off guard, but there was no time to react.

"Let's go," said someone with disgust behind us. "Soon they will bring up the Strangling Jewess and within an hour they will build a whole army out of other phantoms."

We turned around with surprise.

Behind us stood Ledvina, with his bowler hat pushed back and his hands in his pockets.

"Excuse me?"

"In the eighteenth century the Strangling Jewess was the mistress of a monk from the monastery of St. Nicholas," the inspector explained. "But the local abbot sent the monk away and the unhappy woman strangled him in the heat of passion. A few days later she died and is reportedly still wandering around the streets of the Great Market Square. A fairy-tale, just like the Golem."

"Yes, the police ridicule everything," said the rabbi, who had heard us. "I wonder if you wouldn't prefer to see all of us six feet under!"

The crowd grunted and turned slowly towards us with hostile shouts.

"There is no talking with these people," said Ledvina pulling us away. "Come before they throw rocks at us."

We heeded his warning and hurriedly departed before the crowd became violent.

"How did you find us here?" asked Holmes when we were safely around the corner.

"Where else could you possibly be than at the scene of a crime, Mr Holmes?" said Ledvina. "The chief sent me here to get you."

"The chief?" I said. "Does that mean we are in trouble?"

"On the contrary," said Ledvina shaking his head. "The trouble is all ours."

XI

Will the Famous Detective Help?

"I have a problem, gentlemen," said the Prague chief of police quietly.

It was less than an hour later and we were in his office. A picture of Emperor Franz Joseph hung on the wall.

Holmes smiled. It was not the first time he had heard a highly placed figure utter these words.

"How may I be of service?"

The chief blushed.

"Our country is not flourishing, gentlemen," he began. "The people are growing restless. Jews, Germans, Czechs... we all share this small space and coexistence is not easy. I dare say that it is largely due to pressure from Vienna."

"From Vienna?"

The chief drummed his fingers nervously on the desk and fell silent for a moment.

"We Czechs are a proud nation and subjugation to Austria-Hungary does not sit well with us," he said, glancing at the likeness of the emperor on the wall. "The Hapsburgs refuse to admit it, but if something does not happen soon the empire will tumble like a house of cards."

"All of Europe is simmering with tension, not just Prague and Vienna," said Holmes.

"You are right, but I must do everything to ensure that Prague does not become the catalyst. The last thing I need is civil unrest. We have enough on our hands with anti-Hapsburg anarchists and I don't want the Jews to get all riled up too. The murder in the cemetery must be solved at all costs!"

"Your police officers are no doubt more than qualified."

"Naturally," said the chief proudly. "I stand by my men through thick and thin!"

"Then I do not understand what it is you seek from me," said Holmes, lighting his pipe.

The chief rubbed his curly beard and looked at the detective impishly.

"But it is elementary, my dear colleague," he said in the haughty tone that I was accustomed to hearing from my friend. "As you have just seen, lawmen are not exactly welcomed with open arms in the Jewish ghetto, which I suppose is understandable. The Jews are bitter and do not want to cooperate. Finding the killer under such conditions is extremely difficult."

"Meanwhile the clues will become fainter and fainter until one day they disappear altogether," said Holmes.

"Correct, time is of the essence," said the policeman. "And now that they've latched onto their bizarre fable about the Golem they don't even see the murder as a crime, quite the contrary!"

"Do you think that we will have better luck than your men," I asked.

"Yes, doctor," the chief nodded. "At least that is what I hope."

Holmes silently puffed on his pipe and thought. A few days ago he had struggled with boredom in London, now, when fate had called him to the very centre of continental Europe, it seemed that he did not know which case to pursue first. As he never abandoned a case that he had already started working on his priority was still the search for Kuzmic, no matter how dull this seemed in comparison with the brutal murder.

That is why he now hesitated over whether to grant the chief's request. Frankly, even I was unsure what Holmes would choose to do. From the psychological point of view, however, I was glad that the more occupied his mind would be with work, the less susceptible he would be to thoughts of the opiate. On the other hand, the strain that accompanied the current investigation weakened him and made him more vulnerable.

Inevitably, however, his natural sense of justice prevailed.

"I will be happy to help you," he said after pondering the matter silently for a few moments.

The chief was visibly relieved.

"The police will of course be at your full disposal. As an outsider you will have a great advantage of perspective and I have no doubt that your investigation will be a success."

"I will require all your files..."

"Naturally, you will have access to everything."

"I would also appreciate having a person to whom I can turn in case of unexpected problems; a kind of liaison officer, if you will."

"Inspector Ledvina is waiting for you outside," said the chief with a smile.

"In that case there is only one thing left for us to do," said Holmes, doffing his cap and heading towards the door. "And that is to return to the investigation."

* * *

Ledvina was delighted by his new assignment.

He led us straight to his office, which he usually shared with several other police officers, but was now deserted. His favourite bowler hat and coat hung on a peg by the door.

"It's not Scotland Yard, but we have some basic comforts," he said.

He offered us two battered chairs and quickly picked up several fat stacks of documents from the messy desk.

"Comfort softens the brain, inspector," said Holmes dryly. "In this respect, Scotland Yard is not the example one should follow."

Ledvina laughed jovially. He rummaged in a drawer and pulled out a dossier.

"There isn't much at the moment," he admitted. "Only a few facts are certain. The body was found a little after four in the morning by a witness who heard screams from behind the wall of the cemetery. Our men arrived at the scene around five."

"Almost an hour after the crime?"

"It took a little while for the witness to report the case to the station."

"I see."

"The investigators searched the crime scene but did not find any footprints that would help them identify the perpetrator. The doctor concluded that the death was caused by strangulation; the autopsy and a detailed report will follow in the afternoon. The victim was not raped. We will also examine samples of fabrics and skin that we found under her nails. She had nothing on her, just a few coins and a handkerchief."

"Did your detectives find anything at the scene of the crime that could have belonged to the dead woman?"

"Do you have anything specific in mind?"

"The first thing I noticed was that a ring on the index finger of the left hand was missing."

Ledvina looked into his papers and shook his head.

"No, there is nothing here. It was still dark, but we would certainly not miss something like that."

Holmes sighed.

"But you saw the lacerations on her body in the dark, did you not?"

Ledvina noted the hint of sarcasm in Holmes's voice. From his desk he pulled out another document, thickly covered with illegible handwriting.

"According to our examination they are mostly minor injuries that she suffered while defending herself from the murderer. These are around the neck and face, when he tried to gag her to stop her from screaming. But there were a number of other lacerations on her body that she suffered earlier. According to the doctor someone beat her often."

Holmes and I exchanged glances. The results of the medical report confirmed the detective's theory.

"Do you know the identity of the victim?"

"Yes," the inspector continued. "Her name is Anna Vavrova. She was a prostitute and a petty thief. Age nineteen, residing in the Zizkov district, Prokop Square. She was not married, but she lived with a male friend. We know nothing about him as yet."

"I will take care of that," said the detective, rising. "May I take a look at the documents?"

Ledvina handed him the files and Holmes examined them for a few moments.

"Very well," said Holmes when he had finished reading. "May I meet your witness?"

"Of course, I had her brought over to the station," said Ledvina. "She's an old friend!"

* * *

We followed Ledvina through the corridors of the police headquarters, which were located only a few hundred yards from our hotel. It occurred to me that the police chief had specifically arranged our accommodation there in order to keep a close eye on us. The police headquarters itself took up a whole building, but it had neither the hustle and bustle of Scotland Yard nor the elegance of the French headquarters. The Prague headquarters was simply functional.

The lobby was full of people. Some had come to report thefts or assaults. Others, like our witness, had been brought in by the police and were waiting to be questioned by the investigators.

A bearded young man was sitting handcuffed on a bench at the far end of the room.

"Death to the Habsburgs!" he shouted drunkenly. "To hell with the Emperor!"

"He's lucky that a Czech policeman picked him up rather than some Austrian bureaucrat," said Ledvina. "The Emperor does not take kindly to criticism. He could have faced ten years of hard labour in the mines."

"The chief was not exaggerating about the political situation," said Holmes.

"Is he dangerous?" I asked.

"Him? No, don't worry; his bark is bigger than his bite. That's the anarchist Pick. He sleeps here at the station about once a week. But the chief doesn't need to know."

Ledvina winked at us conspiratorially and opened the door to the next room.

"In any case that drunkard will soon calm down and fall asleep."

Sara Mandelbaum had also calmed down.

It was the woman who had spoken to the crowd in front of the cemetery. She now sat in the empty interrogation room and looked around inquisitively. Without the support and strength of her community all combativeness had left her.

"So we meet again, Mandelbaum," said Ledvina when he entered the room, which smelled strongly of the woman's sour sweat.

The woman glared at him and hunched her shoulders.

"What do you want from me?"

"To start with, how about a little respect for an official," Holmes coughed in lieu of a greeting.

Mandelbaum looked at him as though he were from another planet, measuring him from head to toe. She then bestowed the same attention on me. Her mouth was agape, revealing her decayed, yellowed teeth.

"These are the two fellows that were snooping around the cemetery!" she exclaimed.

"The gentlemen are detectives from England. They will be helping us with the investigation."

"Please," she cried. "They can't catch the Golem. None of you can!"

Holmes waited politely for the two of them to stop bickering. Then he stepped closer to the chair where the witness was sitting and looked her directly in the eyes.

"That girl..."

"A whore she was!" the woman spat.

"Do you not want her killer to be punished?" he asked.

Mandelbaum did not answer. She looked away and wiped her nose with the back of her hand. Then she cleaned her hand on her grubby skirt and started squeezing the hem in confusion.

"You hated her so much?"

"Well..."

"What did she do to you? Is it because of how she made her living? You said that she seduced your husband."

"Seduced? If only that was all! I'd have slapped him silly, but in the end I would have forgiven him. Men will be men. But she destroyed our lives!"

"What happened?"

The woman glared at us furiously.

"An addict," she uttered. "That awful whore turned him into an *addict*."

She uttered the word with such disgust that the hair on my nape bristled. Holmes's eyes widened. All that I had done to make him forget his problems fell away like a scaffold made of matches.

"Do you mean drugs?"

"Yes. Laudanum, morphine, opium, hashish… I don't know what else he took from her."

Holmes licked his lips nervously, but then collected himself and continued the interrogation.

"How...?"

"She was not from our neighbourhood, but she had been walking the streets here for quite some time," said Mandelbaum.

"Every decent woman spat at her, but she kept coming back. Everyone always said that as soon as she realised there was no work in the ghetto she would bugger off back where she came from."

"But that didn't happen."

"No. Something else happened. My husband started acting strangely. He didn't come home. He was moody, always in a rage. And then sometimes he acted as though nothing interested him, paid no attention to anything or anybody. Or he started stealing money from me, money for the children's food and for the house. At first I didn't know how or why. I found out only months later. One day I followed him like a bloodhound. She was selling it to him!"

"She was not just a prostitute but a dealer," I said.

"It was like the eighth plague, except that we were not guilty of anything," said Mandelbaum. "My husband was not her only victim. I tried to cure him; I tried to prevent him from going to see her, but he beat me. Finally he hung himself."

She broke down in tears.

"I think we have our motive, gentlemen," said the inspector.

"The circle of suspects has narrowed," I said, placing a consoling hand on the sobbing woman's shoulder. "The killer was apparently compelled to act by the same demons that led your husband to kill himself."

"It is not so simple," said Holmes, sweeping away my conclusions. "Everyone in the Jewish ghetto hated that woman."

"But we did not find any drugs on her body," said Ledvina. "Perhaps it was stolen by some crazed soul who needed drugs and didn't have any money."

"No," Mandelbaum cried. "I tell you that I saw him! It was nobody from this world! It was the Golem who rid us of that accursed woman!"

"What did he look like?" asked the detective.

113

The woman inhaled deeply and launched into the same litany that she had recited in front of the synagogue.

"I saw it only from a distance, from the gates of *Beth Chaim*. It was dark, but it was the Golem. Tall, massive, horrifying! Its eyes glowed red and when it crushed that girl's neck it just snapped. She fell straight to the ground."

"Any details?" asked Holmes. "Facial features, hair colour?"

"Like I said, it was dark. And the Golem doesn't have a face or hair."

"What were you doing out there so late at night?" asked Ledvina.

She shrugged her shoulders.

"A single woman must work to feed hungry mouths, inspector. I work in a pub in Old Town and I was walking home. Then I heard her cry. The rest you know."

"I see," said Holmes licking his lips. I could see that he needed some fresh air. "Unless my colleague objects I think that you can go. I only ask that you do not leave the city so that we can contact you if necessary."

Mandelbaum nodded and Ledvina let her go.

As soon as she had left the inspector turned to my friend and offered him a cheroot cigar.

"Could *she* have killed her? Perhaps she is lying. It could have been jealousy or revenge."

"I don't think so," said the detective.

He accepted the proffered cigar, lit it and closed his eyes as he inhaled the tobacco.

"It's not that she did not have sufficient incentive. She had a motive and opportunity; but women kill differently. She was not strong enough for such a fight, and even if she were, she would have had at least the same number of bruises as her adversary. The dead woman had skin under her nails. But Sara Mandelbaum's hands and face are unscathed."

114

"We have to find Anna Vavrova's companion, and the person she was selling drugs for," said the inspector.

"Perhaps he is the same person," I said.

"You are positively brimming with ideas today, Watson," said Holmes, puffing on his cigar. "But she was just the last link in a long chain, a mere cog in a giant machine. She will soon be replaced by someone else, and we must get to the centre of this intricately woven web. With luck this will lead us straight to the killer."

XII

Complications that Simplified Everything

Holmes and I stood on the banks of the murky Vltava River. An icy wind was blowing. Beneath our feet lay the dead body of Mr Kuzmic. He was covered in fallen leaves, blown over here from the other side of the river.

"The plot thickens," said Holmes dryly.

He studied the gaping wounds on Kuzmic's face with distaste and at the same time morbid fascination.

"The gulls did a number on him before we found him," said Ledvina. "We estimate the time of death at eight in the morning."

"Is it really him?" I said, peering at the dead man's rigid and mutilated face. The features were barely recognisable.

"This is indeed Michal Kuzmic," said Holmes. "Look at the scar on his mouth. That is from my whip. And he is wearing the same ring that he wore in Paris. Your people are correct, inspector. Thank you for calling us."

"So the chickens have come home to roost," said the inspector. "But why?"

The body had begun to rot. I placed a handkerchief in front of my face and looked at the horizon.

"The cause of death was the large gunshot wound in his neck," said Holmes, crouching over the body, which he had turned onto its side.

"An execution?" said the inspector.

"Yes," Holmes nodded.

He rummaged through Kuzmic's pockets. His search revealed nothing and he let the body roll back with a thud.

I shuddered with revulsion.

"The knees of his trousers are frayed, which supports your theory," Holmes said."Otherwise the trousers are new. He was clearly kneeling before he died."

116

He stood up and wiped his hands with a handkerchief.

"A sad ending," I said.

Kuzmic was a fraud and a liar, but he had not deserved this.

"How did he bring this upon himself?" asked Ledvina, as though reading my thoughts.

"Maybe someone became alarmed when I was asking about him in the Poison Shack," said Holmes, stroking his chin. "Or perhaps it was Mayer."

It was our second dead body in less than twenty-four hours. But this murder also meant the end of our original investigation. At least I saw no way to recover the stolen money from the dead man. But Sherlock Holmes was tenacious.

"Our journey may have changed course, but we have still not arrived at the end," he said.

"What shall we do?"I asked. "Shall we go after Mayer? Or the Golem?"

"What would you do, inspector?" the detective asked Ledvina.

Ledvina consulted his pocket watch and frowned. It was already almost four o'clock.

"I suggest we finally have lunch," he replied.

* * *

It was dusk.

As we walked through the hilly, rundown streets of the Zizkov district, where we planned to visit the late Anna Vavrova's lover, the darkening sky was even greyer than during the day.

This appalling neighbourhood was where Holmes had decided to continue the search. As he rather cynically said, Kuzmic was not going anywhere, while the case which fanned unrest among Prague's Jews threatened to escalate into a far more serious incident.

We ascended some steps to a little tree-lined square from which led several streets. According to the inspector's records this was where the murdered woman had lived with her lover. Due to the missing ring, at this point he seemed to Holmes the most likely suspect.

In the middle of the square there was a small newsstand. The owner was just closing up shop and putting away the papers. We walked over to her and Holmes greeted her politely. She looked up at him briefly and continued her work. The clock on the column showed one minute after six.

"We're closed," she said brusquely.

"We don't want to buy anything," said the detective.

"So what do you want?"

We were not accustomed to such rudeness. But Holmes was always willing to treat a woman politely. He took a few small coins from his pocket and placed them on the counter.

"May I buy some tobacco?"

The woman grumbled, but went inside the booth and a moment later reappeared with a packet of tobacco. She held out her hand in expectation of payment, but Holmes did not have it.

"This is snuff, madam," he said calmly. "I smoke a pipe."

The woman looked at him with murder in her eyes and again plunged into the bowels of the booth. She returned with a package that even I could smell.

"That is my favourite," said the detective and he gave her a banknote.

"Do you have smaller bills?"

"Keep the change," said Holmes.

This coaxed from the woman a servile smile. The pathway to her heart was now open.

"Do you know Anna Vavrova?" Holmes asked.

"You mean the young girl who lives around the corner?"

"Yes."

"I don't pay attention to other people's business, I have enough work of my own," she said, shrugging.

But she leaned out of the window a little more in order to take a good look at me as well.

"She is a good girl, but a little flighty," the woman continued." She lives with her man in an awful ground floor flat in that building. She says she works in a dressmaker's shop, but I have my doubts. She walks the streets at night doing God only knows what. But it's no surprise, because that man of hers is a good for nothing who doesn't have a job, drinks and steals her money. And when the poor girl doesn't have any, he won't think twice about smacking her about. Today he was already drunk at noon. He could barely stand up; he almost walked into my stand! It won't turn out well, believe me. I've already seen it. But like I say, I don't know anything about her. I'm not a gossip who sticks her nose into other people's business."

She had revealed everything we needed to know.

"Thank you, madam," said Holmes.

"Any time, gentlemen," she cried after us as though we were her best customers.

Then she slammed the window and closed the shop.

A few minutes later we were standing around the corner in front of the ghastly tenement building that the woman had pointed out. The five-storey building was covered in grime, the plasterwork was cracking, and most of the windows were broken.

The gates were unlocked and a dingy corridor led from the entrance through an inner courtyard to Anna Vavrova's flat. A draft whistled through the corridor and made the doors rattle.

I shuddered with repulsion.

"Does he already know about the death of his mistress?" I said. "Have the police notified him?"

"If he killed her, then he knows about it," said Holmes.

He knocked on the door of the apartment. There was no answer and he tried the doorknob. The door swung open and we entered cautiously.

I could not have imagined a more dreadful abode. The filthy room was empty save for a few wretched pieces of furniture. The walls were mouldy and the floor and ceiling were damp.

A body lay immobile on the floor.

"Is he dead?" I asked.

"No," said Holmes, feeling the pulse on the man's neck. "Just drunk."

"Good heavens!"

"His lover is dead. If he is indeed the killer he might be suffering pangs of conscience. But we won't find out until we wake him."

"Should I make coffee?"

"I know a better way," said Holmes, kicking aside a bottle lying at his feet.

He sat the torpid man up and slapped him twice in the face. As a man of medicine I objected to this method, but it was infinitely quicker than the solution I had proposed.

The drunken man gurgled and his eyes slowly peeled open.

He was probably about thirty-five, but appeared older. Life had not been kind to him. His unshaven face was covered in burst veins and his blue nose and cheeks made him look almost like a caricature. But beneath all that he actually had quite handsome features. He was dressed in worn corduroy trousers and a filthy shirt. The odour of cheap alcohol emanated from his mouth.

"What is it?" he said squinting at us.

He wanted to get up, but his body would not listen. We helped him into a chair and poured him some water in a tin cup.

Once he had swallowed it he looked at us with a slightly less bewildered expression.

"My head hurts," he said.

But if he was looking for compassion from Holmes all he got was an icy stare.

"What do you want here?" he said suddenly. "You're cops, right?"

"Yes," the detective nodded. "We need to speak with you."

"I didn't steal anything. Have a look around. It won't take you long."

He coughed violently and waved his hand at the bare room.

"That's not why we're here," said Holmes.

"We came because of Anna Vavrova," I interjected. "I'm afraid we have some bad news for you."

"If that whore stole something from you, you won't find it here."

"Unfortunately, we have to inform you that Miss Vavrova is dead," I said.

"What?" he cried, jumping up. "It's not true! It can't be!"

His reaction seemed genuine, but Holmes had a much more deeply rooted distrust of people than I had. He had uncovered countless frauds and charades and was not easily duped.

"She was strangled," said Holmes mercilessly." Probably on account of a theft."

"Who could do such a thing?" said the man. He dropped back into his chair and put his head in his hands.

"What is your name?" asked Holmes, putting his hands on the armrests and leaning towards him.

"Franz Svejda."

"Where were you last night between midnight and six in the morning?"

"Here. I was sleeping."

"Can anyone confirm that?"

"No..."

"Well, Mr Svejda, it may come as a surprise to you that you are the prime suspect," said Holmes.

"Me?!"

"Yes. According to the forensics report Anna Vavrova was frequently beaten. By you!"

The man turned pale and shook his head feverishly.

"No, no, it wasn't me! I mean, maybe I taught her a lesson once or twice...You know women; it's the only way they'll listen!"

Holmes shook his head in disgust and turned away from him.

"What do you know about her work?"

"What work?"

"Don't lie! You know how she made her money. Did you force her to do it?"

"I never forced her to do anything! She was already working the streets when I met her. One of her customers did her in, you've got to believe me!"

"I'm not talking about prostitution!"

The confusion on Svejda's face simply could not have been simulated.

"Then what?"

"Don't play dumb! She was dealing drugs!"

The man gasped.

"Where did she get them? Who organised it?"

"I swear I have no idea!" Svejda cried.

He suddenly seemed quite sober. I was becoming increasingly convinced that he was speaking the truth.

"Don't lie! You lived with her, you must have known!"

"For God's sake, I'm telling you the truth! I had no idea she was involved in something like that!"

"Where do you think she got the money that you stole for your liquor? By selling her body? Don't be funny! You killed her, and in the end you even stole the only valuable thing that she had in the world! Where are you hiding it? Where is the ring?"

"In the pawn shop," said Svejda.

"You killed her and then sold the ring!" the detective cried in triumph.

"No, no! She sold it herself! Yesterday afternoon. I needed money for something, I promised her that I would return the money as soon as I could and buy back the ring. We argued a little and, yes, I hit her, but Anna sold it herself! She didn't believe me. Then she went into town and I drank the whole night. I got drunk and then you woke me up."

Holmes and I both froze.

"I didn't kill her. I loved her!"

Then he broke down and began to cry.

"Do you have proof of your assertions?" Holmes asked.

Svejda rummaged in his pocket and pulled out a crumpled pawnshop receipt. It was dated yesterday and signed by Anna Vavrova.

"I swear, I didn't do anything," he said tearfully.

So much for the motive. Holmes abruptly turned on his heels and we left.

The broken man knew even less about his mistress than we did.

Outside darkness had fallen and a pall seemed to descend over my friend as well.

Svejda obviously had not killed her. We now had to seek out the killer in the murky waters of the Prague underworld.

It was something I had sincerely hoped Holmes would not have to do.

XIII

Warning

Holmes went to bed early that evening. He was tired and perspiring. The day had not been an easy one. I sensed that he was again fighting with his inner demons, trying to dispel thoughts of the opiate, which thanks to the case had returned to him now at this most inopportune time. Ever since our meeting with Miss Watts I had hoped that work would help him through the worst, but now it seemed quite the contrary. I could only pray that he would win his battle.

These thoughts troubled me during dinner with the Countess. I wanted to apologise on behalf of myself and Holmes for not paying her any attention that day.

To my surprise the Countess was in a good mood. She accepted the news of the death of Kuzmic without visible sign of grief, and so after dinner we ventured out into Wenceslas Square and to a café which had an unrivalled collection of billiard tables.

The pleasant evening extended well into the night and I slept in rather late the next morning. When Holmes woke me just before noon the first thing that occurred to me was that he had not slept a wink. His face was creased and he had bags under his eyes. But he insisted that he felt all right and all he needed was a walk. So we went outside.

It was a frigid day and the cold wind made us shiver.

We walked from the Adria Hotel to the lower end of the square in the direction of the river. The stately boulevard that we walked along was full of beautiful buildings, which Holmes discussed excellently. I was not surprised. He sometimes relaxed his great brain by filling it with miscellanea.

During the walk we also discussed both of our cases from all possible angles. Holmes told me that in the evening he would again head to the Poison Shack to collect more information.

By now we were in the Great Market Square. In its centre was a half-built monument to John Hus, the Czech spiritual leader who had been burnt at the stake for his heresy. Apparently this square was now where demonstrations against the Empire were staged by anarchists like Pick, the drunkard we had seen at the police station.

We were now getting very cold, so we decided to take a carriage the rest of the way.

As if by divine providence at that moment an empty carriage pulled up next to us. The horses were scrawny, but the carriage was attractive and clean. The driver sat on the seat, bundled up to his nose in a shaggy shawl over which shone a piercing pair of eyes. For a brief moment I thought they looked familiar, but the cold wind drove the idea from my mind.

"Do you want a fare?" the detective asked, and when the driver replied in the affirmative we took our seats.

The carriage set off and we swayed comfortably. We threw a warm, red-checked blanket over our knees. Passing by the Hus monument we circled the whole square.

We travelled at a leisurely pace and meanwhile the detective had launched into another description of some building or other. His words soon began to blend together and lost all meaning for me. I nestled more comfortably in the warm blanket. My eyelids drooped and I drifted into sleep.

Bang!

I was startled awake as though by cannon fire. I fell back and almost did a somersault. I did not know what was happening.

Above me a pair of horse's hooves flailed in the air. The animals screamed with terror. The driver was standing on the seat, cracking his whip above his head in a mad effort to hold on. I was afraid that the animals would fall and crush me.

Holmes was trying desperately to untangle himself from the blanket. I must have been asleep merely for a few seconds, because we were still at the town hall. Around us people were shouting and converging on the carriage.

"What happened?"I stuttered. "Has someone shot at us?"

"No, our rear axle burst," said Holmes. "Quickly, we must get out of here!"

The driver shouted and the horses broke into a gallop, pulling the broken carriage forward with a sharp jolt. The rear wheels had completely fallen off, and the carriage bounded and scraped along the cobblestones sending sparks flying into the air, which frightened the horses still further.

While the driver was ready for the jolt and stood firmly in the seat, Holmes, still struggling with the blanket, fell and hit his chin on the edge of the carriage.

Blood flowed but I could not help him, because the headlong rush of the animals pushed me back into the padding and prevented me from moving.

The people who had gathered in front of us were now fleeing in every direction. The driver balanced wildly on the seat and tried to rein in the horses. My hat flew off and disappeared. The world around me was like a blurry streak of colours and terrified and screaming faces.

After a while I stopped perceiving sounds. A strange silence pervaded me. All I could do was hold on tightly and pray that the driver would settle the horses and stop the carriage before disaster struck. Sparks were flying everywhere.

The horses circled the square, the carriage tossing this way and that behind them.

Someone cursed. Holmes was conscious.

We had now left the market square and had careened into a side street leading to another much smaller square. In the centre stood a gushing wrought iron fountain and around it a raucous crowd was milling among canvas stalls selling fruit, bread and fish.

Even in their madness the animals no doubt realised that they could not fit into this tight space and so tried to push between the fountain and the houses. But as the horse swerved, the coach skidded and buried itself into a wall with a thunderous crunch. Unfortunately it was the window display of an ironmonger's shop and so I suddenly found myself in the midst of fragments of broken glass, rubble, dust and small iron utensils.

The horses screamed and snorted, but the carriage was firmly wedged into the house and would not budge.

People ran over and tried to help us but as soon as they moved me I felt a pain in my arm. The impact had broken my arm. I pushed the people aside and looked for Holmes, but he was no longer in the carriage next to me.

I scrambled up with the help of my good arm and rolled out onto the pavement.

Someone was holding the horses and calming them. A policeman approached. People flocked from the stalls. A few bricks still fell from the wall shattering what remained of the glass display window. Someone tried to make me sit down on the edge of the fountain, but I was looking for my friend.

I pushed my way through the crowd. My eyes were full of dust, which made my eyes water.

Holmes was lying motionless on his stomach in a broken vegetable stand. His head was covered in blood. He must have fallen out of the carriage during that last sharp turn.

I felt almost like fainting, but I knelt near him and took his head in my hands. He groaned and opened his eyes.

"Don't move, you're injured," I said.

I shouted to the onlookers to immediately call for a wagon. Holmes had to go straight to the hospital.

The detective frowned and touched his head. His fingers were sticky with blood. He looked at them uncomprehendingly, probably in shock.

Then he licked his fingers curiously.

"Tomatoes," he said, glancing at the price tag next to him. "A little overripe, I must say. I certainly won't be buying them at this price."

At first I did not understand. I thought he was delirious from the blow to the head. It was only when he stood up, dusted himself off and began to wipe the tomatoes from his head that I realised he was truly all right. At first glance the only injury that he had sustained was a cut chin. We could be thankful that the accident had not ended up worse.

By now a crowd of onlookers had formed around us. A policeman was dispersing them and assessing the damage.

Holmes and I returned to the carriage in order to check on the driver.

But to our surprise we did not find him.

"Have they already taken him to the hospital?" I asked the policeman.

"Who?"

"The driver," I said, pointing to the broken carriage in the shop window.

"He disappeared," said the policeman. "He's probably afraid that he will have to pay the damages. But we'll find him by his licence, don't worry sir. Will you want to file a complaint?"

That thought had not even crossed my mind. My primary concern was for the poor fellow's well-being.

Holmes meanwhile was examining the carriage, from which the horses had already been untethered. He swung himself into the seat. It contained a whip and a small rucksack.

"Come here, Watson. You will find this interesting."

He handed me the rucksack. It was full of money. Bundles of banknotes, a veritable fortune.

"Who can it belong to us?" I cried.

"Us," the detective replied, showing me a note attached to the rucksack.

It was a message from the carriage driver.

THIS IS THE MONEY THAT KUZMIC STOLE.
THERE'S NOTHING ELSE FOR YOU TO LOOK FOR
HERE, HOLMES.
LEAVE.
YOU HAVE BEEN WARNED.

I was so flabbergasted that I inadvertently leaned on my broken arm. I yelped with pain.

"It seems that Kuzmic's killer wants us out of Prague as soon as possible," said the detective. "Apparently that is why he killed him. An interesting turn of events."

"Why must he deliver his message so theatrically? Why doesn't he wait until we leave?"

"He must be planning something big and is afraid that I will learn about it and present an obstacle. He was even willing to part with all of this money. Apparently we are stepping on his toes."

"Do you mean our investigation into the murder of Anna Vavrova?"

"Correct," said Holmes. "That is the only thing that makes sense."

I was happy that it occurred to me without his help and I blushed.

"Our two cases have merged beautifully," said the detective.

I sat on the edge of the fountain and shivered. I was literally drenched in sweat.

"Watson, you are injured!" said the detective. "Forgive me for ignoring you. You must go at once to the hospital!"

"A splint will suffice," I said, but I did not feel at all well.

The shock had subsided and the body was taking its toll. A woman put my coat over my shoulders and a policeman gave me a cup of water.

Then fortunately an ambulance arrived and took me and Holmes to the hospital.

* * *

"You seem drawn to wild carriage races, Mr Holmes," said Ledvina jovially.

We were in the hospital, where the doctor had put my arm in a plaster cast and sewn two stitches on Holmes's chin.

The detective turned away from the mirror, in which he had been examining his stitches, and looked at the inspector sullenly.

"I assume that the chief will want you to keep a closer watch over my investigation," he said scornfully. "No doubt he concluded by saying *I told you so*."

"Not at all," laughed Ledvina. "It was not your fault, after all. And personally I am glad that you destroyed an ironmonger's shop instead of a pub."

"My pleasure," the detective replied, and he began to dress.

The nurse brought me a sling to hang my broken arm in and the policeman pulled a greasy notebook from his breast pocket.

"We have already begun the search for the carriage driver who vanished so mysteriously."

"Excellent. Have you found him?"

"Not yet."

"I had assumed not," said the detective. "This person will certainly be hiding. Our unknown friend left us a warning note in the carriage and all of the money that Kuzmic stole from our clients in London."

He showed Ledvina the rucksack full of money.

"So it wasn't an accident?"

"No. I suspect that a thorough inspection of the wreckage will reveal that the broken axle was in fact cut. Everything was ingeniously planned."

"You think that he wanted to kill you?"

"No. The accident was doubtless intended as a warning. Otherwise he would not have returned the money."

The inspector looked at the note.

"This explains why we could not find the licence for the carriage or its owner. Do you know what the driver looks like?"

"He wore a scarf," I said.

"It is not much to go on," said Holmes. "No, my dear Watson, we must get to the middle of this criminal web in another way!"

XIV

Decoy

Holmes may have devised a plan, but it was not enough. In order to carry it out he needed several important ingredients, chief of which was the Countess, who was to play a key role in the resolution of our two connected cases. But she did not take at all kindly to our proposal.

"If I understand you correctly," she said," you want me, in all seriousness, to be a *whore*?"

"I like that you call things by their true name," laughed the detective, who was not as shocked as Ledvina to hear her use such language. "Nevertheless, I only need you to *pretend* that you are a lady of loose morals so that we can ensnare the killer."

Holmes, Inspector Ledvina, the Countess and I were sitting at the best table in the Gottwald Café, which thanks to its cosiness and excellent coffee had become our headquarters during our stay in Prague.

"I don't know whether to be amazed or insulted," said the Countess, leaning back in her chair and swallowing a glass of port.

"There is no other woman in Prague whom I could ask to do this. You are the key to the success of our mission."

"Well, when you put it that way it sounds a little better," she said. "But what if something should happen to me? It is too dangerous."

"My men will be at the ready the whole time," said Ledvina. "If Mr Holmes is right, you will be approached by someone who will try to remain inconspicuous. He will not be able to risk using violence."

"That's reassuring. How do you picture the whole thing then?"

Holmes folded his long fingers together.

"With the brutal murder of Miss Vavrova the octopus has lost one of its tentacles," he said. "There is no doubt that her murder is directly connected with her involvement in the drug trade. Now the missing member must be replaced. A new angel of addiction will surely be sought from the same pool of candidates, the *filles de joies.*"

"And you want to throw me to the octopus?"

"I would favour another solution if I knew of one."

"Why don't you just apprehend some other poor woman and use her?"

"We cannot arrest every single prostitute in Prague and determine who works for Mayer and who does not. It would take a long time and we would draw too much attention to ourselves. We must act quickly, purposefully and discreetly."

"All right, Mr Holmes, I will do it," said the Countess. "It's the least that I owe you."

She gracefully held out her hand for him to kiss.

"We will be nearby the whole time and I promise that the whole thing will go smoothly," said the detective standing up enthusiastically. "We begin tonight."

"In that case I suggest that the Countess spend the morning with us at the station," said Ledvina. "Our men can show you a few manoeuvres to ward off a possible physical attack."

"I think that I know how to defend myself against pushy men."

"These men are different than any you have encountered before," said Holmes."They are truly dangerous and cannot be shaken off. They lack all sense of decency and compassion. Traders in narcotics are the cruellest of all criminals."

"Yes, you can never be too careful," I said. "We would not want you to come to harm."

"Don't worry, we will take care of you at the station," said Ledvina reassuringly.

The last part of our discussion had again planted doubt in the Countess's mind, but she did not want to go back on her word. We toasted the success of the mission and after that she seemed to lose all fear and asked to return to the hotel. She needed to get some rest before her big day. A much greater adventure awaited her than she could have ever imagined when she first met us aboard *The Sprinter*.

But we still had much to do.

For Holmes's plan to work, and for the culprit to take the bait, we had to make him feel safe. As long as we were in Prague he was unlikely to emerge from his hiding place.

So that evening we made a great show of checking out of the Adria Hotel and boarding the night train to Paris with all of our luggage. Before departing we had a light supper in the station restaurant and made sure that we were seen on the platform. Holmes watched carefully to see whether anyone was following us and when he was satisfied we boarded the train. Inspector Ledvina rushed down from the newspaper office, where he had delivered the message about our imminent departure, to bid us farewell.

The whistle blew and the conductor came to check our tickets. Ledvina waved to us from the platform as the train slowly pulled out of the station.

Meanwhile a shadow watched our departure from a dark corner of the railway yard.

* * *

Early the next morning we met the Countess and Inspector Ledvina in the lobby of the Adria Hotel.

In the middle of the night a police wagon had driven us from the first stop outside of Prague back to the city. We had then snuck through the rear entrance back into the Adria Hotel. We had not gotten much sleep, but in the Afghan war I had often times slept even less.

Despite the early hour and a clearly perturbed mood, the Countess shone with natural beauty. She wore a beautiful dress, which as she had explained to me earlier she had ordered from the best tailor in Prague. She was visibly proud of her taste. We could not have chosen a more beguiling temptress to play the part of our decoy.

Holmes, Ledvina and I were to accompany the Countess to the police station, where she would be instructed in self-defence. Meanwhile we would collect the results of the autopsies that had been performed on the bodies of Michal Kuzmic and Anna Vavrova.

"Good morning, madam," said Ledvina to the Countess. "We have a lot of work ahead of us today. I can see that you have even put on your costume!"

The Countess froze.

"Excuse me?"

Before we could intervene Ledvina continued with his folly.

"Your dress. I could not have picked it better myself. It is just the kind of vulgar thing that the ladies in the Poison Shack wear."

Outside it began to thunder and rain. The Countess's face clouded.

"It is not a costume, inspector; this is my evening dress."

Beads of sweat formed on Ledvina's forehead and his chin trembled. His usually rosy and plump cheeks turned pale and he took a step back.

"The carriage is waiting, gentlemen," said the hotel valet, saving the poor inspector. "May I offer you an umbrella?"

Ledvina breathed a sigh of relief.

The Countess took cover beneath the umbrella and darted past the inspector, swiftly kicking him in the shin with the tip of her high-heeled shoe as she passed.

She did not talk with us the whole way and did not even say goodbye when we arrived at the police station.

Holmes and I spent about two hours at the station, mostly with the coroner. Alas, he did not have good news to report. The autopsies only confirmed some of Holmes's conclusions from the preliminary examinations. The bits of skin and fabric under the girl's nails were inconclusive. We only learned that the skin was most likely from the attacker's soft tissue, perhaps the neck, and that the fabric could have been from any woollen garment.

We had also left the recovered banknotes to be examined. They were unequivocally genuine, unmarked, and did not originate from any robbery.

It seemed that our blue-blooded decoy was the only way out of this dead-end.

We went to the police gym, where the Countess was practising self-defence manoeuvres. We watched the exercises for a little while, during which the delicate Countess d'Ambolieu demonstrated several impressive tackles and throws.

"When I see you in action all my worries disappear," said Holmes.

"Thank you," said the Countess breathing heavily. "But I hope that it won't be necessary. After all you will always be nearby."

"Yes, most of the time," said Holmes.

"What do you meant *most* of the time?"

Holmes and Ledvina exchanged glances.

"We agreed that one of you would always have my back!"

"In the field yes," said Holmes. "But we need our man to take you all the way to his boss. You will need to go with him all the way to their hideout."

"The hideout of those insane murderers!" she cried. "Not a chance!"

"That is why we will equip you with something else too," said Ledvina. "We wouldn't want them to catch you with your pants down!"

So saying Ledvina led us down to the basement of the police station. The lowest floor, deep beneath the surface, was a complex labyrinth of rooms and secret chambers. The vault into which he led us looked like a mad scientist's laboratory.

"Welcome to the kingdom of Sergeant Kvasnicka," the inspector whispered when he opened the door. "This is where we prepare for cases that require, ahem, a special approach."

"What do you mean?" I asked.

Ledvina looked at us mysteriously and seemed about to tell us, but was interrupted by a carefully coiffured man in a white coat and bowtie. He was distinguished-looking and mysterious, just like the laboratory itself.

"You can chat outside," he said curtly, emerging from behind a complex set of glass flasks. "Now we have work to do. The chief sent you here so that I can help you succeed in the mission, right? Or perhaps I am mistaken?"

"This is Sergeant Kvasnicka himself," said Ledvina, leaning on the table.

"Please do not touch anything with your greasy hands, inspector!" Kvasnicka cried slapping the inspector on the hand. "This is an aseptic environment! Come, Mr Holmes, let us begin the presentation."

He led us all into the depths of the underground laboratory, which was full of bizarre devices. Ledvina stood banished at the entrance.

"Here you will receive some implements that will increase your chances of survival in the field."

"I hope that I will not have to learn to use any complex devices, gentlemen," said the Countess.

"Not to worry, my dear," said Kvasnicka condescendingly. "We recently developed some things especially for the ladies."

On the counter to which he led us there was placed several seemingly ordinary items: a polka-dot umbrella, a lace handkerchief and a lipstick.

Holmes picked up the umbrella and studied it with interest.

"This is supposed to help me?" said the Countess. "Should I hit him with it?"

My friend smiled faintly, winked at Kvasnicka and swiped elegantly with the umbrella at my top hat, which I was holding in my hand. A dagger shot from the tip of the umbrella and sliced the decorative ribbon.

The Countess and I gasped. Kvasnicka looked pleased.

"Excellent, you have a keen eye, sir," he said pointing to the miniature lever with which Holmes had released the knife. "Thanks to my modified umbrella the attacked can in the blink of an eye become the attacker."

The Countess grasped hold of the umbrella with new enthusiasm and attempted the same manoeuvre that Holmes had done. She must have once had fencing lessons, because she brandished the weapon with bravura and grace, as though the blade were a natural extension of her arm.

Up next was the lace handkerchief.

"The handkerchief secretly contains pepper and smoke capsules," said Kvasnicka, carefully unfolding the lace and showing us two artfully mounted capsules. "All you have to do is wave it in front of an attacker's face and the fragile case will break and release its contents."

"Most extraordinary!" I exclaimed.

But the Countess was much more interested in the lipstick.

"The stick is made from sugar cane. If you see something suspicious, pretend that you want to put on lipstick, then bite off the tip, swallow it and it becomes a whistle that you can use to signal for help."

"The criminal's last kiss will truly be sweet," said the Countess.

"That's not very funny," said the sergeant, taking the lipstick away and closing the case. "It might save your life, and it is also very tasty. I have a whole box of them."

"Ingenious inventions, Sergeant Kvasnicka," said Holmes slapping him on the shoulder. "A man with your talents would be of great use to our secret service."

The inventor flushed happily while we all marvelled at his brilliance.

We would soon find out just how much these devices would come in handy.

* * *

The Countess stood in the middle of the Jewish ghetto in front of the synagogue.

Wearing a dress that truly did resemble the one sewn by her Prague tailor, a blonde wig and provocative makeup, she was practically unrecognisable. Holmes and I along with a unit of men in uniform led by Inspector Ledvina were concealed behind the cemetery wall and watched through several gaps in the masonry. We were just a few paces from the scene of the murder, the tomb of Golem's creator. It silently reminded us all why we were there that day.

Our decoy played her role to perfection. She sauntered up and down the street, loudly greeting the outraged men who passed by in an adorable French accent, winked at them, swung her hips and occasionally adjusted her fanciful hat and waved the deadly umbrella. For all intents and purposes she appeared like the most experienced courtesan. Had I not known who was hidden beneath the costume I would not have recognised her.

It was getting late and we had already been waiting a long time. The men, who were not allowed to speak or smoke, were getting restless. There was nothing to amuse us, but we had to keep on watching attentively so as not to risk some danger befalling the Countess. The only sound was the rumbling in the stomach of the poor inspector, who apologised with a guilty laugh.

It was dark now and the Countess moved beneath one of the old gas lamps at the wall of the synagogue. I nervously fondled the revolver in my pocket. I had been carrying it ever since the night's adventure at Thorpe's house.

Shortly before midnight several men approached the Countess. Ledvina recognised one of them as a prominent member of the imperial secretariat. But our lady drove them all away. They were just lechers, lusting after their fleeting bodily gratification.

Holmes, Ledvina and I took turns watching the street. When he was not on watch, the detective walked among the tombstones, searching for something. He apparently still hoped to find some other clues to the murder.

At one point he stooped down to pick up something in the darkness. He studied it for a long time, but I could not tell what it was. Then Ledvina nudged me with his elbow and I turned away from Holmes. Either he threw away the find or put it in his pocket, but when I looked again he was already hurrying toward us with long strides to see what had caught the inspector's attention. He did not mention what he had found so I assumed it was nothing important and immediately forgot about it.

Much more interesting things were happening in front of the synagogue.

Wheels clattered on the cobblestones and an ornate-looking black coach pulled up to the curb. The doorknobs and ironwork shone gold in the yellow light of the lamp and the black horses shook their lush manes and stamped their hooves on the pavement.

Alas, the coach blocked our view of the Countess. We could only guess what was happening behind it. A pair of legs in tall boots appeared between the wheels. The unknown man walked over to our lady and stood next to her for a few minutes.

We could hear only her impassioned babbling and the man's deep voice.

It had to be our man.

Ledvina whispered instructions and the unit silently boarded the police wagon what was positioned at the ready. We had to follow and stick by the Countess at all costs. If we lost her we likely would never see her alive again.

It all happened so quickly that my heart almost stopped. The Countess climbed into the unknown man's coach and it jolted forward. Holmes and I scrambled into the wagon and passing through the cemetery gates we set off in pursuit, keeping a safe distance behind.

We were closing in on our prey.

XV

Elementary, my Dear Watson!

The streets were as quiet as death. Our wagon moved like a shadow after the Countess and her mysterious client. Were it not for the lanterns on the coach in front of us, which led us like a torch through the dusky ghetto, we would have been lost. But we soon left the ghetto behind and were slowly heading to the more prosperous part of the city.

Holmes was silent the whole way. His condition continued to worry me. Whenever he seemed to have put the worst behind him his withdrawal symptoms returned, with varying levels of intensity. I was at my wits' end and prayed for the conclusion of this unhappy case.

Ledvina peered out of the bouncing wagon and whistled.

"Whoever this man is he isn't poor," he said. "Look at those villas!"

He was right. The suburban area in which we now found ourselves was filled with palatial homes, streets planted with trees and paved with light stone. It was called Vinohrady, named after the royal vineyards established on these hillsides centuries ago during the time of Charles IV.

"Inspector, they have stopped," the coachman whispered.

Holmes quickly stood up.

"Indeed," he said.

Quickly as a cat he jumped down from the wagon.

Ledvina and I got out behind him and took cover in the shadow of the wagon.

The Countess and the mysterious man had just gotten out of the coach next to a three-storey Italianate villa surrounded by a large overgrown garden. A light shone in the second floor windows. A curtain parted slightly and a shadow peered out.

The late visit was expected.

The man led the Countess to the gate. He pushed her impatiently and walked close behind. Before entering the house he looked around furtively to make sure nobody was following him. In the light of the door we caught a glimpse of his face.

I caught my breath. It was Kuzmic!

Holmes recognised him too and squeezed my arm. How was it possible?

A day earlier we had seen his dead and mutilated body. Suddenly I realised why the eyes of the carriage driver had seemed so familiar to me.

It had been him!

But what about the Countess? She must have nerves of steel to be able to continue the charade! Or had Kuzmic recognised her? If yes, then her life was in grave danger. We could no longer be certain of anything.

We waited until the door closed behind them.

"What nerves!" Ledvina whispered admiringly.

"Hell hath no fury like a woman scorned," said Holmes.

"Do you know who that house belongs to?" said Ledvina. "Your friend Rudolf Mayer. Several times already we have searched it, but we never found anything."

Holmes looked as though he had seen the ghost of Professor Moriarty.

"We can't put anything on him, even though he's the biggest fish in the pond," Ledvina continued. "In Prague not even a pickpocket will steal without his permission. The chief has already given up all hope of solving the case."

"I believe that we shall catch this fish today," Holmes said with a sly smile. "Maybe even the whole pond!"

"If you catch them for trafficking and for the murder of that prostitute you will get a medal."

"I think, therefore, that it is high time to cast the net. Gather your men!"

The men quietly jumped from the wagon and gathered at a nearby wall. They were armed with sabres and rifles. The inspector ordered them to encircle Mayer's house, but they had to remain silent in order not to reveal our presence. The Countess and our friend still needed time to talk.

Once the men had surrounded the dark building the deadly noose was in place. All that was left to do now was ensure that it tightened around the right neck.

"What now, Mr Holmes?" said Ledvina.

"I will take a look inside," said the detective. "As soon as I give you the signal your men will storm the house and arrest everyone!"

"But it is too dangerous!"

I could only agree with the inspector. The detective had not told me of his intention, knowing full well that I would protest. The original plan had been to leave everything to the Countess, allow her to enter into Mayer's service, and only charge the house as soon as she was safely outside.

But there was no time to argue. Holmes anyways ignored our objections and like a tiger honing in on its prey made a break for the house. He flashed past the fence and leaped into the garden.

He had already disappeared from our sight when I realised that he had not taken a gun.

"Damn it," I cursed.

"What is it?" asked Ledvina.

I told him about the gun, but he waved his hand dismissively.

"Your friend's greatest weapon is his brain."

But a brain, even the best one, cannot force an enemy to drop his gun or put his hands over his head. But the revolver in my pocket could.

"I must go after him," I said.

"What about your arm, doctor?" asked Ledvina.

But trying to stop me was just as futile as trying to stop Holmes. I had to help my friend and the Countess.

As the street was only dimly lit I succeeded in penetrating the garden unobserved, just as Holmes had. My arm proved to be a handicap when climbing the fence, but not an insurmountable one. Ignoring the pain I braced myself against a brick pillar and just barely managed to clamber over the wall. I peered into the darkness in front of the house, where the lawmen were quietly waiting.

Then I headed deeper into the garden.

It took a little while for my eyes to accustom to the darkness. Now I could make out numerous garden beds, shrubs and trees. The grass glistened with moisture, thanks to which after a while I could see footsteps leading to a basement window. It was open, as though inviting me inside.

I took a deep breath and slid feet first into the darkness.

Someone grabbed me by the ankles and pulled me down sharply. I was so frightened that I had no time to scream. I landed on a pile of coal and quickly rolled over on my stomach. The revolver fell out of my pocket.

I tried to reach for it with my good arm, but my assailant kicked it out of my reach. He grabbed me from behind and twisted my arm behind my back. My broken arm throbbed and I yelped with pain. The pressure suddenly subsided.

The attacker turned my head and looked in my face.

"For God's sake, Watson," said Holmes. "What are you doing here?"

"You forgot to bring a gun," I panted. "I brought it for you."

For a moment it looked as though my friend would keel over.

"I thought that you were one of them," he said. "It seemed to me that someone was following me, and when you started to climb into the basement..."

"Don't apologise, I am all right," I assured him. "Fortunately the plaster held."

"Do you realise that I might have killed you?"

I did not know what to say.

"I couldn't let you go without a gun," I explained, catching my breath.

I was black with coal dust. Holmes was not much better off, but we could not ask for a better mask for our night ambush.

The detective picked up the revolver and stuck it in his belt.

"Thank you," he said, squeezing my shoulder gratefully. "Once again you have shown me that fortune could not have blessed me with a better friend and associate."

His thanks were the greatest compliment.

"Should I go back?"

"No," he said, shaking his head. "We were fortunate that nobody saw you. It might not happen a second time. It will be better if you stay with me. But stay behind me and don't do anything."

The cellar in which we found ourselves was surprisingly small for such a large and opulent house and did not contain as many items as one would expect. Except for a pile of coal, a wooden ladder, an oil lamp and an empty wooden bookshelf there was nothing here at all.

Holmes took a wax candle from his coat pocket and lit it. The wick took a while to catch but then flared obediently, illuminating the room with its flickering glow.

"If we cover the window to the garden then maybe we can also light the oil lamp," I said, pointing to the oil lamp hanging near the stairs.

"It's not light that I want," said Holmes, looking thoughtfully at the walls and ceiling.

"Then why did you light the candle?" I said in bewilderment.

Holding the candle, Holmes walked along the wall containing the bookshelf and ran his hands over it. He was looking for the hidden entrance to a secret room!

"Ledvina said that a search of the house revealed nothing," he said."We know what Mayer is up to. This is where he hatches all of his schemes. No doubt this is where he and Kuzmic planned the London robbery as well as his fake death, which was designed to throw us off the trail. He must have a hiding place here. And as you have no doubt noticed, the size of this cellar does not correspond with the dimensions of the villa. I believe that there is definitely a lot more here than meets the eye!"

The flame of the candle flickered and blew out under a weak draft which came through a crack in the bookshelf. Now that he knew where to look it only took him a few moments to find the hidden button that opened the entrance to the secret room. The wooden wall of the cellar parted to the side and Mayer's kingdom opened up before us.

I gulped.

At the far end of the room there was a massive safe, like the ones banks have. It was probably full of the valuables that Mayer had collected over the course of his criminal career.

But Holmes was much more interested in the wooden crates that stood arranged one on top of the other. He picked up a crowbar that was lying on the ground and began to pry one open. The wood cracked, the nails gave way and the lid creaked open.

The crate contained small marked packages of opium, morphine, cocaine, heroin, hashish; every conceivable drug. As a physician who occasionally used these substances to treat my patients, I could immediately recognise the evil that such a supply of intoxicating poison could unleash. And there could be no doubt about its non-medicinal purpose. The price that it would probably command on the black market was staggering.

Holmes's eyes glazed over and the crowbar fell from his hand with a thud. He began to shake violently and I had to brace him from falling. The sight of the opiate was making him lose all self-control.

I did not know what to do. Poor Holmes almost fainted in my arms.

"I told you we would meet again, Mr Holmes," said a voice behind us.

I whirled around. The shining eyes of our undead friend, Mr Kuzmic, were again fixed on me.

"I should have known your departure was a ploy," he said.

He was pointing a gun straight at us.

"The boss won't be happy with me. But what will happen to you will be much, much worse."

* * *

When Kuzmic led us upstairs Holmes was in a total delirium. He practically let himself be carried. He just stumbled along and did not pay me the slightest attention. His eyes were listless and were it not for his breathing I would not have known that he was still alive.

Kuzmic pushed us in front of him and stuck the barrel of his gun in my back. Had Holmes been in his right mind he certainly would have remembered the revolver in his belt, but in his current state the weapon was just as effective as if it were locked away in my bedside table in Baker Street.

After all our adventures, after all of the powerful enemies that we had defeated, I could not believe that cocaine would be what brought the brilliant detective to his knees! But at that moment coming to terms with this nightmare was the only thing I could do.

Kuzmic marched us out of the cellar. Several fearsome-looking members of Mayer's gang were sitting in the kitchen drinking coffee mixed with rum. Kuzmic barked something at them in Czech and continued with us upstairs.

"Aren't you supposed to be dead?" I asked, hoping to distract him so that Holmes could mount a surprise counterattack.

"You would like that, huh?" laughed Kuzmic. "I hope that you enjoyed our little theatricals. But no, you had to keep on meddling! Don't be surprised now if the truth hurts. Just like it hurt that dupe when our quack doctor modified his face so that he could take my place on the riverbank."

But my effort was in vain. Holmes just stared numbly ahead.

Mayer's house was opulently and expensively furnished. Thick carpets, crystal chandeliers and valuable vases decorated the hallways through which Kuzmic led us.

We then entered Mayer's office, where the man himself sat enthroned on a gigantic leather chair.

He was an enormous man. He had a massive bald head with beady eyes and meaty lips that smirked over fat jowls. His expensive tailored suit probably consisted of as much fabric as Mrs Hudson had used for our curtains. In one hand his thick, sausage-like fingers grasped a glass of brandy and with the other he stroked the knee of the Countess, who was seated next to him.

When he saw us he leaned back even further in his chair and crossed one leg over the other. For a moment he gazed at me and Holmes expressionlessly and then drank calmly.

"The famous Sherlock Holmes from London and his loyal associate Dr Watson," he said, toasting us.

"They were in the cellar," said Kuzmic, poking Holmes between the shoulder blades.

The detective lurched forward and fell at Mayer's feet. He was so weak that he could not even pick himself up. I was not permitted to help him.

He was clearly in a trance brought about by a fresh paroxysm.

Mayer looked at Holmes's coal-covered figure with disgust and pulled away his shoe to avoid soiling his white spats.

"They were sniffing around the safe, and they found the merchandise," Kuzmic continued.

"What did they see?"

"Everything. This genius then collapsed. I didn't even have to knock him about."

"Too bad for them," said Mayer and he bent over to the Countess who was sitting with her knees pressed closely together. "Forgive me, my dear, I have to interrupt our interview for a minute. But don't go anywhere. You can watch."

But the Countess had no intention of running away. At the moment she looked just as paralysed as Holmes. She had coped with the shock of discovering that her fiancé was a fraud like a true lady and had not flinched when she learned of his supposed death. But his resurrection, when he picked her up in front of the synagogue, was too much for her. What a reunion it must have been!

Mayer set aside his glass and rose out of his chair.

"So this poor wretch bested you, Michal?" he said sarcastically. "But to be fair there is something to his reputation. My good friend the late colonel Moran always spoke of him with fear. And it killed him."

"Moran was a weakling," said Kuzmic.

"Probably," the criminal boss nodded and squatted on his haunches near Holmes. "There's no other way to explain how this wretched fellow got him."

"Enough!" I cried.

Were it not for my broken arm I would hit this ugly good for nothing right in his pudgy face.

"All around the world criminals and murderers like you tremble at the very mention of his name!"

"Criminals and murderers? Like me?" said Mayer.

"Yes, your reputation precedes you, Mayer," I said spitting.

"Your friend's too," he said winking. "Today we will confirm it."

He stood up and nodded to the Countess to join him. She rose obediently as though in a daze. I could see how confused she was. Moreover she knew nothing of Holmes's cocaine habit and therefore did not have the faintest idea what was happening. I hoped that I would yet have the chance to explain it to her.

"But we have been so rude, Michal," said Mayer, walking to the bar cabinet. "Our esteemed guest deserves to be given that which he most desires. And you, my beautiful bird, can learn something about your new occupation."

From the bar he took out a silver case and brought it over to Holmes.

"This is a lesson in why you should never misappropriate my merchandise. Otherwise you will end up like this poor wretch."

"What do you intend to do?" I cried. But Kuzmic held me firmly in place.

"You will assist me," he said to the Countess. "Roll up my sleeves."

Mayer opened the case and removed an empty syringe, tourniquet and a bag containing several grams of cocaine. He handed the tourniquet to the Countess.

"Find a vein."

It was clear to me now what he wanted to do.

"You can't do that!" I cried. "It is worse for him than death!"

"Elementary, my dear Watson," Mayer smiled and he gave Holmes a contemptuous kick.

There was nothing I could do.

XVI

Dead End

I stood as though anchored in place and watched as Mayer readied a death for Holmes worse than hell itself. There was no blood, no threats. The obese criminal simply held the deadly syringe, smiling villainously. He turned Holmes over on his back and brought over an oil lamp. My blood boiled and I experienced the whole scene in slow motion, as though each second were an hour.

The poor Countess still did not know what was happening and had to continue playing her role. Mayer gave her the rubber tourniquet and she wound it tightly around the detective's bicep. A few purple veins protruded from his forearm.

"Why are you doing this?" I cried.

There was nothing else I could do. Kuzmic was still holding me firmly and with my broken arm I had no chance of breaking free.

"You ask me why I am destroying your friend's life," Mayer said disdainfully. "That's not a fair question. He has already destroyed it himself. Look!"

He pointed at Holmes's bare arm. On one of the protruding veins several needle marks were now clearly visible.

I could not believe my eyes. Where could they have come from? I had relieved his withdrawal paroxysm with an injection only once, on the first night in Paris after the chase. The other needle marks, and they were numerous, he must have made himself, and Mayer did not have to tell me where they probably came from. But as far as I was aware he had not had access to cocaine since we left England. And my medical bag, from which he might have taken something, was locked away untouched in my hotel room!

At that moment I felt deeply ashamed for Holmes, more than I ever had before in my life. He had deceived me and lied to me. But I could not be angry with him.

"Once an addict, always an addict," said Mayer. "That is our business model, after all, doctor. In the last moments of his life the famous Mr Sherlock Holmes will return to the path along which he has long treaded. There is no more elegant death."

Fate had played us a bad hand.

Mayer removed the glass cylinder that was covering the oil lamp. He measured out several doses of cocaine onto a spoon and placed the spoon over the flame to melt the drug. Then he drew the liquid into a large syringe.

Now even the Countess understood what was happening. She grew pale and looked at me desperately. But Mayer interpreted it as excessive sensibility.

"Don't flinch now, my dear," he said. "If you want to be in this business you need to have a strong stomach. Hold his arm!"

The Countess pushed away Holmes's arm defiantly.

"I won't do it!"

"If you don't you will be sorry!"

"Are you going to kill her like you killed that poor woman in the cemetery?" I cried. "She also refused to do your bidding and so you got rid of her!"

"What nonsense are you spouting?" said Mayer. "I didn't do anything to any woman in any cemetery!"

"She was one of your dealers! You cannot deny it! After all, here is her replacement whom you have recruited!"

Mayer looked at me in astonishment.

"I deny nothing, doctor. You deserve to know the truth before you die. True, I am looking for a replacement. But why would I kill her? That girl was good, one of the best. I don't know who killed her, but it definitely wasn't me!"

"So your lackey killed her!" I said, turning to Kuzmic.

"Do you mean Michal here, this ungrateful sodomite?" the fat boss growled in disgust. "I gave that boy everything to disappear after that incident in London! He was not supposed to return ever! But he squandered everything with his recklessness, and when things took a turn, he had the audacity to come back here, and with you in tow! And at the worst possible time for my plans. He almost ruined everything! Now I keep a close eye on him and if he wants more money he will have to earn it."

"But what about that warning?" I cried, while Kuzmic momentarily loosened his grip. "Was it not meant to discourage us from investigating the murder?"

"I repeat that I had nothing to do with the murder of that whore," said Mayer. "I returned that English money to you so that you would go away. My business here is worth millions and my partners get nervous when the world's most famous detective comes snooping around. But you are mistaken about that murder. You should have heeded my warning."

Judging that it was enough talk the scoundrel now placed the deadly needle on Holmes's arm.

"Wait!" the Countess cried. "At least let him die with dignity!"

"What do you mean?"

"This man is a legend, he must not die in tatters," she said winking at me and she started fixing Holmes's dirty shirt and tie. "May I wipe the soot off his face?"

"All right, but be quick about it," growled Mayer with the needle at the ready.

The Countess pulled a white lace handkerchief from her bosom. It was the one that I had last seen on the table in Sergeant Kvasnicka's laboratory.

Before I, Kuzmic or Mayer could blink, she unfolded it and then threw it into the face of the surprised fat man.

"What the hell?" he cried, but then the secret weapon began to work.

The villain stumbled and dropped the needle. He had to close his eyes, which watered and burned from the pepper cloud. Then there was a bang as though from a cannon.

It was Holmes sneezing. He had inhaled a little of the Countess's pepper and it had brought him around. He lifted himself weakly and groped about, but he still did not know who or where he was.

"Grab that woman!" yelled the blinded villain, who was rubbing his eyes furiously.

Kuzmic let go of me and lunged at the Countess.

From the belt under the coat of the dazed detective she pulled out my revolver and hit Mayer with the butt on his bald forehead. He collapsed and knocked over the oil lamp. The flaming oil spilled out onto the carpet and immediately caught fire.

But now the devil Kuzmic had dug his fingers into his former fiancée's neck and began to brutally choke her. The gun flew somewhere under the chair and disappeared from our sight.

"Holmes, help us!" I cried and grabbed Kuzmic from behind.

The detective was now on his hands and knees and was slowly coming to.

He must have thought he was in hell.

The carpet was on fire and the fat villain was wallowing on his back, unable to open his eyes. The Countess was wheezing as her strangler tightened his grip and I was latched onto his back, trying desperately to dislodge his hands.

Holmes groped in front of him and grabbed the lethal injection which Mayer had dropped. He gazed at it as though he had found something he had long sought. He was coming to; I could see it in his eyes. But I also saw something else there, something that I feared more than a whole gang of Mayers and Kuzmics.

He craved the drug. The desire was so overpowering that it had already compelled him to forget everything and everyone.

He needed it. His greatest struggle was not with Moriarty, but right here and now in this room, with himself.

I cried out again. I don't know what I said; at that moment the words were of little consequence. I felt the futility of my actions, despair over our depraved lives. If Holmes were to succumb now, nothing else would matter.

Now Kuzmic finally recognised the Countess. Her wig had fallen off and the heat had melted her makeup. He smiled wickedly and tightened his grip further. His handsome face transformed into that of some twisted and horrible demon as he brutally strangled his beautiful victim.

I hit him again and again on his back, but he shook me away like a fly. With each second the Countess was losing her life.

Suddenly my friend's pupils began to focus. He looked at the injection of cocaine in his hand and squeezed it hard.

Then he rose up, darted at Kuzmic and plunged the needle into his neck. The fiend wheezed, let go of the young woman and fell backward. He began to writhe on the floor next to his boss, who was slowly coming to.

It was not a pretty sight.

The flames were already licking the furniture and curtains. The room filled with black smoke and stifling heat.

Suddenly the sharp sound of a whistle pierced through the smoke. It was the Countess blowing on Kvasnicka's lipstick!

The sound also brought Mayer to his feet. He looked around wildly and hurled a torrent of Czech expletives at us.

Kuzmic crawled to his feet and implored him, hand outstretched in a deadly delirium. But his boss, lover, guardian or whoever he really was kicked him into the flames and stumbled out of the room.

There was no longer any helping the fiend. He was engulfed by the blazing inferno.

Through the crackle of burning furniture I heard Ledvina's men breaking through the door downstairs and fighting with Mayer's henchmen. Someone screamed and a gunshot rang out.

The retreat to the cellar was apparently barricaded, and the head of the underworld had no choice but to flee to the attic.

I guided the Countess out of the burning room and into the cooler air of the corridor. But Holmes was still inside. I feared that he was too weak and that without my help he might not make it out alive.

I had to go back for him.

He was standing amidst the flames like a phoenix rising from the ashes. He seemed to be looking for something.

"Holmes, we have to go!" I cried.

"I'm looking for your revolver, Watson," he replied.

"To hell with it! Come or we will burn!"

"I have to go after Mayer. And I need a weapon!"

"Why? He ran upstairs and can't get out!"

"If the fire does not go out and he is burnt to death I will never get the answers to my questions!"

"We have them," I said. "When you were unconscious he told me everything."

Holmes turned towards me, but did not move. He seemed unperturbed by the flames licking at his heels.

"He confessed?"

"Yes and no," I said. "Mayer is behind the drug ring and he had Kuzmic's double killed because of us. But apparently not the girl."

"That is puzzling," he said, frowning. "From what we know it is clear–"

"Holmes, I implore you, come out at once and I will tell you everything!" I cried, losing all patience. "The Countess is waiting for us on the stairs. We need to get out!"

Finally he relented and came out with me into the corridor. The Countess was holding her scarf over her nose and mouth and was eagerly awaiting us.

"I was getting worried!" she cried.

Holmes gallantly kissed her hand.

"May I borrow your umbrella, Countess?" he asked.

"Certainly."

"Take the Countess downstairs, Watson. I will join you directly!"

Then he turned on his heels and ran up the stairs, where he vanished into the smoke.

"That damned fool!" I cried, but there was nothing else I could do.

I escorted the Countess to the ground floor, which the men had already secured. The battle with Mayer's bloodthirsty gang had moved into the cellar and the garden.

Ledvina stood at the main entrance with a gun in his hand and a bloody gash on his face, but otherwise he was all right.

"Wait for your friend outside until it is finished," he said to me. "The fire wagon is already on its way. And we'll get those criminals who barricaded themselves downstairs soon enough."

"The cellar is full of drugs," I told him. "In a secret room behind the bookshelf."

"I knew it!" the inspector cried. "Mayer can't get away now. And it is all thanks to you. But where is Mr Holmes?"

"He ran upstairs after Mayer," said the Countess.

"I will go after him," I said. "He will need my help."

The young woman and I exchanged glances. Nobody except us must know what had happened upstairs and the other demons that Holmes needed to contend with besides Mayer. Not even the friendly inspector.

"Go, doctor," said the Countess. "He needs you."

I kissed the marvellous woman on the cheek and brandishing the pistol that Ledvina had pressed into my hand I ran back to the upper floors of Mayer's villa to help my friend in his last battle.

The fire had already spread to practically the entire attic. But I only realised this once I had ascended the staircase. At that moment the banister behind me became engulfed in flames, cutting off the way back.

* * *

I opened the door to the attic and just managed to duck as the broad side of an ancient sword whooshed over my head.

"Watson, take cover!" Holmes cried.

Upon entering the uppermost floor of the house I became a witness to an extraordinary fencing duel. Rudolf Mayer had been chased like a rat into a corner. He was soaked in sweat and in his massive hands he clutched the hilt of a two-handed broad sword which he had evidently taken down from the wall. Against him stood the slim and wiry Holmes, brandishing the polka-dot umbrella, from whose tip the sharp dagger point protruded.

"It's all over, Mayer," I said, levelling Ledvina's pistol at him.

My hand trembled as my finger reached for the trigger.

"No!" Holmes cried. "Don't shoot! This is between us!"

Mayer's fleshy lips formed into a malevolent smile.

"You have signed your death warrant!" he cried, lunging at the detective.

How could the thin umbrella withstand the heavy blows of the broadsword? But the detective elegantly fended off the attack and sent Mayer reeling back. Later I learned that the umbrella was made of the strongest steel.

This enraged the criminal even more. He executed an exhausting series of thrusts, his obese body darting this way and that with surprising dexterity, but Holmes deftly fended off every attack. I could only marvel at his strength and skill.

I hid in a corner behind a stove and watched the action unfold. It was a sight I would never forget.

The flames had now begun to appear in the door to the attic. I closed it, but dense smoke wafted through the crack above the floor, making us cough.

"Be reasonable, both of you!" I cried. "We will suffocate!"

They did not listen.

All that mattered to them was their ferocious duel.

When the air had become so thick that they could hardly see, Mayer grabbed the heavy stove behind which I was crouching and sent it hurling through the window. Shards of glass flew into the night sky and a gust of fresh air blew into the attic.

But the draft also blew open the door to the attic and fanned the flames that were now entering the room. Our lives were in grave danger. The flames began to spread to the beams and the roof.

Holmes and Mayer fought on.

Sparks flew from their swords. They shouted at each other furiously until spit flew from their mouths, evaporating in the white-hot air before it could hit the ground. The fire chased me from my hiding place and the only place I could safely go was behind Holmes, who fended the lunges of the desperate criminal away from my head.

I wondered what we would do even if Holmes should win.

There was no way out. Perhaps it would be better to perish at the hands of Mayer than burn to death.

The giant was now weakening. His weight and the heat proved to be just as formidable opponents as the detective. Holmes pounded Mayer's sword with the umbrella like a hammer banging on an anvil. Finally the exhausted Mayer failed to cover one of his thrusts and a subsequent kick from the detective sent him staggering.

He lost his balance and fell backwards.

The fight had brought all of us right to the edge of the broken window. Mayer's arms flailed wildly in an attempt to grasp at something and before Holmes or I could do anything, with a shriek of surprise he tumbled out of the window.

We heard his sword land with a crash in the shards outside.

But Mayer had managed to grab hold of the gutter and was clinging to it for dear life. He could not hold onto it for long, but there was enough time for us to reach him.

"Give me your hand, Mayer!" said the detective.

But he was hanging outside of his reach. Perhaps if I held onto Holmes's legs he could lean out further, but with my broken arm I was powerless to help.

Beneath us the policemen were running hither and thither and shouting at each other.

Ledvina was feverishly looking for something that Mayer could land in.

But it was futile.

The dying criminal looked down and knew that he could not survive the fall. His luxurious villa was burning; the flames had already reached the cellar where his drugs had been incinerated.

His eyes filled with sadness.

"You should have heeded my warning," he said. "But I swear I did not kill her."

Then the gutter loudly ripped away and Mayer with a dull thud landed next to his house.

Holmes and I looked down. A stream of blood ran from the kingpin's head into the burning grass.

"Do you believe him?"

"Men do not lie when they are at the threshold of death," said Holmes.

We now found ourselves alone in the highest floor of the burning building. There was no escape.

I realised that this was the end and that there was nothing to do but say goodbye.

"I lost, my friend," the detective whispered hoarsely. "I let you down, I know. And what's more, I have led us into a dead end."

I wanted to reply, but the smoke was suffocating me and all I managed was some wheezing.

And then the floor fell out from under us.

XVII

The Fall

The epicentre of the fire was in the second floor, but we fell all the way to the ground floor kitchen. Fortunately for us it was one of the few in the house still free of flames. As if by a miracle neither of us was seriously injured in the fall. Yet when the floor gave way and the walls and beams shattered around us I was convinced that my time had arrived.

After the policemen helped us from the rubble the pace of events slowed. The fire wagon arrived and began extinguishing Mayer's house – or rather what was left of it.

But Holmes's mind still burned with the question of who killed Anna Vavrova.

It was late and we were deadly tired. The Countess had succumbed to shock and was trembling uncontrollably. She kept recalling the horrors and dangers from which she had so narrowly escaped. The doctor examined all of us. Holmes and I had light burns on our faces and arms as well as several abrasions.

We arrived at the hotel in the morning and immediately went to bed.

But the worst day of my life was about to start.

Even now, as I write these lines years later, the memories send a chill down my spine.

I was the first to wake up. Looking at the clock near my bed I realised that I had slept eighteen hours! My arm ached, but the burns on my cheeks had ceased to sting. Outside it was raining heavily and the drops drummed on the windowpane.

My stomach was growling, so I arose and dressed with the thought of getting something to eat from the hotel kitchen. It occurred to me that Holmes would be hungry too, so I went to his room to see if he would join me.

He was still asleep with his head nestled deeply in the pillows.

I was not surprised. He had suffered experiences that I would not wish on my worst enemy. I felt guilty for being unable to protect him from his addiction. I was torn between remorse and anger. How could he have been so weak? Why had he again succumbed to his addiction after he had come so far? No doubt he had obtained drugs during his night at the Poison Shack. What a fool I was not to have noticed it!

The room was an ungodly mess.

His personal belongings were strewn around the bed and there was a mound of items on the table. The dresser drawers were all open and his suitcases were overflowing with the costumes and accessories that he used to disguise himself for his clandestine trips.

I do not know what compelled me to start cleaning. I had never done it before. Perhaps I never should have done it in the first place.

As I was folding Holmes's tattered coat, the one he had worn the night before at Mayer's villa, something fell out of the pocket. It was a scrap of fabric. It must have been the thing that he had found in the cemetery while we watched the Countess. A shiny button was stitched to it, which was probably how he had seen it in the darkness.

It must have belonged to the murderer, I thought to myself. I was pleased that Holmes now had another clue to help him identify the culprit in this last unsolved case.

I finished tidying up the rest of his belongings. All that was left to do was close the suitcase and push it under the detective's bed so that he would not trip over it in the morning.

But something was jamming the lock. I had to rearrange the things inside the suitcase in order to close it properly. A crumpled raincoat lay on top, the one which the detective had worn as part of his disguise the night he visited the Poison Shack.

Then I saw it.

The brown coat billowed in front of me revealing a tear in the fabric. It was the same size and colour as the scrap of fabric from the cemetery. And the buttons on the coat were the same.

I stared in horror. For a moment my mind refused to put the facts together. There must be some mistake.

Golem.

A giant creature made of clay. At night easily mistakable for a tall man in a loose brown coat. Golem, the man into whom Holmes had transformed himself on the night of the murder.

Not a man, but a monster. Holmes had that night transformed into a monster.

Then I remembered the needle marks on his arm and the scratches on his neck, which I had attributed to the chase in Paris. Put the tissue found beneath the nails of the prostitute under a microscope and I would wager that it matched the skin on Holmes's neck.

My God, Holmes, what have you done?

Clearly he had no awareness of the monstrous crime he had committed. He was asleep. Unknowing. When he strangled the girl he had not been Sherlock Holmes but a madman, uncontrollably guided by the craving for the drug. The girl, who must have accosted him in the night, could not have known what a beast she would awaken. At that moment he had to have the drug and strangling the wretched girl and robbing her was the fastest way to get it into his bloodstream.

His body and brain had betrayed him. It was a textbook case of Dr Jekyll and Mr Hyde.

My mind raced furiously.

Holmes knew nothing. His brain had subconsciously refused to join the facts that would reveal the truth. How else could it be explained that he had not yet discovered the truth? I did not believe he would deliberately frustrate the investigation.

It was not in his nature. Had he had the slightest notion of what he had done he would immediately turn himself in.

Then I sensed a movement behind me.

Holmes sat up in bed and looked at me and at the things in my hands. There was no hiding the look of despair on my face.

He froze.

His eyes grew wide with understanding as though suddenly everything were coming together in his mind. At that moment we both knew.

My eyes welled with tears.

I do not know how long we sat across from each other like that. When a person's world collapses he doesn't look at his watch.

Then my stomach heaved. I could not sit there with him staring at me like that. I ran to the bathroom and retched.

I cleaned my face and returned to the room.

Except Holmes was gone.

I had not been in the bathroom more than five minutes! Where could he have gone in this state?

The bed was as he had left it. He had not even taken a clean shirt. His shoes, trousers, overcoat and beloved deerstalker cap were the only things that were missing.

I did not find him in the hallway or anywhere else in the hotel. The night receptionist told me that he had run outside, but could not say where or in which direction he had gone.

I ran up and down Wenceslas Square like a madman. I was probably more afraid for him at that moment than at any other time in our acquaintance.

It was raining heavily and the streets were empty. I searched all the surrounding streets and arcades, peering into every nook. For some reason I even looked for him in the German casino. I went to every conceivable place and everywhere I called for him.

But the only answer I got was the sound of the rain.

My shoes were already soaked through. As I had left in a hurry I had taken neither an umbrella nor a coat. Poor Holmes must have been in the same situation, perhaps even worse.

I had to find him.

I took a coach and went to all the places that I could think of. The coachman must have thought I was crazy. I leaned out of the window and shouted the detective's name at the top of my lungs.

We drove past the Powder Tower and the Market Square, where a few days earlier we had had our wild ride.

Eventually we arrived at the Charles Bridge with its columns of statues.

It was the last place I would have looked for him. But it is where I found him.

Holmes was standing near the middle of the bridge, grasping one of the statues and balancing on the stone edge.

At first I thought that the silhouette belonged to one of the statues, but then it threw off its cap. I jumped out of the coach and ran towards him.

He looked at me.

Rain streamed down his face, mingling with his tears. I immediately understood what he intended to do.

Beneath the bridge black water thundered and shattered against the piers.

"Have you come for a final farewell, Watson?" he said, his voice trembling with emotion. "You should have stayed in the hotel. You have already experienced my death once and today it will be no less unpleasant!"

"Have you gone mad?" I cried. "Why are you doing this?"

"What else can I do?" he said, raising his arms theatrically. "I am a murderer, Watson. There can be no forgiveness. I was overcome by fury and that poor girl was my victim! I became that which I have fought all my life!"

"So keep fighting!"

"How?"

"Just as before! Don't throw away all those years when you used your abilities for the benefit of mankind! We all have skeletons in the closet. Lock yours up!"

"I cannot, my friend, I cannot," he said quietly and looked again at the surface of the river. "I can no longer trust myself. I am a danger even to you."

Then he paused.

"I no longer have the strength," he said.

And he jumped.

I could not just stand there and do nothing while my best friend ended his life. I threw off my jacket and shoes, cried out to the coachman to call for help, swung my arm out of the sling and jumped onto the railing.

The water had already engulfed Holmes.

I closed my eyes, prayed, and hurled myself into the foaming waters of the Vltava River.

The water was excruciatingly cold. But I had to find Holmes.

I dove.

In the darkness I had no chance of seeing anything, so I flailed my arms around in hopes of grasping him. My clothes stuck to me and pulled me downwards, but I kicked my legs furiously and somehow managed to stay afloat.

The longer I looked for the detective the less hope there was of his survival. I thrashed about in a vain attempt to feel his body. I was running out of air, but I'd rather my lungs burst than emerge without my friend. I was at the edge of consciousness, and the natural instinct for survival compelled me to come to the surface.

I took a deep breath and again plunged beneath the water. I was now some distance from the pillar from which Holmes had thrown himself. Perhaps the current had already carried his body, broken by the breakwaters and the rocks, down to the bottom, but I continued to believe that he was still within reach. If only it would stop raining and the moon would come out!

At last my hands grasped on to some kind of clothing and I pulled up with all my might.

It was him!

When I brought his head to the surface my heart rejoiced.

He had not drowned, but his eyes were closed and his breathing was weak.

"Holmes, don't you die on me!" I cried, hoping that for once he would listen to me.

Water was everywhere. It went into my eyes and I swallowed it instead of air. I swam with Holmes to the bank as fast as I could. He needed to be dry and warm, otherwise pneumonia would set in and all my efforts would be in vain.

Finally we reached the bank, but my hopes were dashed when I realised it was a high stone embankment and there was no hope that I could climb up. I clutched desperately at the slippery wet rocks, but it was futile. Then the current dragged us farther downstream. It was all I could do to keep my friend's head above water and stay afloat.

We passed beneath a bridge and drifted farther and farther. I was weakening.

I was overcome by a desire to rest. Holmes began to slide out of my hands, which were numb with cold. But no, I must not let go!

When I suddenly felt solid ground underfoot, I reacted instinctively without realising what it really meant.

A wave had thrown us onto a kind of staircase which led up to the embankment. I grabbed hold of the railing and climbed out of the water. I did not let go of the detective's body for a second. I held him firmly by the shirt collar and dragged him up, summoning whatever strength I had left.

It had finally stopped raining.

I was gasping and I stopped for a moment to catch my breath. Then I pulled Holmes up the stairs and onto dry land.

I left Holmes lying there and ran along the embankment.

The current had washed us a few hundred yards downstream from the Charles Bridge. Above us loomed the dark outlines of the Prague Castle. Somewhere behind a high wall I could hear tumultuous merriment coming from a pub.

I yelled at the top of my lungs for help.

On the bridge I could see the lights of torches moving about in the darkness. They were looking for us, but too close to the spot where we had jumped into the water. It never occurred to them to look so far downriver. I waved my arms to get their attention, but they could not see me in the darkness.

From behind the wall a lantern appeared and someone said something to me in Czech. He did not understand what I was saying, but from my frantic tone he no doubt gathered that the situation was grave.

A gate opened and a man ran out carrying a lantern.

He helped me move Holmes into the house and we wrapped the detective's trembling body in as many blankets as we could find.

I had ripped him from the clutches of death.

XVIII

The Twilight

I told Ledvina the truth.

After everything we had been through together he deserved to learn the identity of Anna Vavrova's killer. I must admit that there was a little selfishness in this too. I did not want to be the only one to bear the heavy burden of the decision about what to do next. Should we report our discovery to the police and let Holmes be arrested? The great detective, whose very name was synonymous with honour and the fight against crime? Or destroy the evidence and sweep everything under the rug as though nothing had happened? Neither of these options seemed right to me.

The good inspector and I thought about this long and hard in the days after Holmes's suicide attempt. The detective had closed within himself and lay recovering in his hotel room. He refused to go out, eat or meet anyone. He was incapable of looking his friends in the eye. I took long walks and often, after his shift was over, Ledvina would take me to his favourite pub.

"Do you know what I think, Doctor?" he told me one day over a frothy pint of beer. "Let's let it be. Rudolf Mayer is dead. We cut off the octopus's head. In time it will certainly grow anew, but at least we have slowed it down. And my conscience is not troubled if one more murder is attributed to Mayer. It is lost among the great number of his crimes."

"But is it right?" I asked.

"Look at it this way," he said philosophically. "Who benefits if we let Holmes stand trial? The press will have a field day. The only ones who stand to benefit are his enemies. Criminals around the world will rejoice. Their greatest obstacle will have been removed. A new wave of crime will break out."

He was right.

"Meanwhile good and honest people will lose an idol," Ledvina continued. "They will lose someone they rely on when they are in trouble. I don't just mean your clients, but everyone who sees Holmes as a symbol of truth. For us he is a man with his faults; but for others he is a legend."

"The great Sherlock Holmes must remain unstained," I said, nodding.

"Yes, let us drink to that," said Ledvina, lifting his glass.

His words made sense. But I still felt that simply sweeping everything under the rug was wrong. Holmes still had to face his weaknesses and make amends for what he had done. He was not above the law.

He had to get better. My efforts alone were not enough. He needed professional help, long-term supervision.

That evening I sent a telegram to an acquaintance of mine in England who owned a specialised clinic. I informed Holmes of my intention as a *fait accompli*. He did not argue with me and humbly accepted what I had arranged for him. Our visit to Prague had ended.

The next day we departed for the train station.

The people of Prague, including the local Jews, had come to bid Holmes farewell. The chief of police was there too. He thanked Holmes for everything he had done for the city and for apprehending one of the most wanted criminals in Austria-Hungary.

If only he knew what defeat was hidden behind this victory!

My friend smiled politely, but inwardly he was crying.

The most heartfelt farewell was with Inspector Ledvina. Over the past couple of weeks this good-natured man had grown close to our hearts and I was certain that the detective's secret would be safe with him.

Then Holmes and I and the Countess boarded the train and waving at the crowd left the city behind.

After a long time we were again alone. Just the three of us, exactly as we had arrived in Prague. We were the only ones who knew what we were bringing home with us.

Outside it was cloudy, but the gloomy weather suited the mood inside the compartment.

"Countess," said Holmes hoarsely after a period of awkward silence during which we had avoided looking at each other. "I want to thank you for everything that you have done. No matter what happened, I hope that you will remain my friend."

It was the first time that he had spoken to her since we had left the burning house.

The Countess smiled and pressed his hand.

"You are a good man, Mr Holmes," she said with tears in her eyes. "I know it, and I will not change my conviction. A terrible thing happened, but we will help you overcome it."

We bade her farewell in Paris. She left the train station with a sad expression on her face and with the knowledge that her revenge on Kuzmic had become in the light of later events somewhat secondary. But the con man had gotten his just desserts and perhaps much more.

Holmes and I spent just a few hours in Paris. We immediately departed for Calais where a ferry was waiting to take us to Dover.

As Holmes and I stood on the deck and gazed at the approaching shores of England it seemed to us as though the whole country had been cast in a shadow of dark clouds. Perhaps it was just our unhappy frame of mind.

We returned the money that Kuzmic had stolen to our clients, Mr Gottfried and Mr Watts. We did not go into great detail about the course of the investigation. Fortunately they were satisfied.

Shortly after our return to Baker Street I took my friend to Kent, where my former schoolfellow now headed a sanatorium for drug addicts. Holmes spent the rest of the autumn and winter in this excellent facility. It was a difficult treatment, but he braved it stoically.

I visited him often and did what I could to help him. But the main task was his and his alone. He did not return to Baker Street.

"From one's past mistakes one learns only that one never learns from one's past mistakes, my dear friend," he said to me during one of my visits, when I asked him whether he had mastered his problems.

It did not sound overly optimistic.

When the treatment was over Holmes bought a country house on the southern slopes of Sussex and retired there. Here, in Cuckmere Haven in Fulworth near Eastbourn he devoted himself to beekeeping. It seemed to bring him peace of mind.

But as for detective work, that chapter of his life was over.

Dr Watson's Postscript

I submitted the manuscript of this case, which I entitled *Golem's Shadow*, to Mr Doyle with contradictory feelings, but with Holmes's blessing. I must admit that in my heart of hearts I was relieved to stop guarding the black secret about Sherlock Holmes's retreat from public life.

To my surprise, the publisher returned the manuscript to me; and not by post, but in person. He was visibly distraught. Clearly he had looked forward to my new case and to the hordes of paying readers who would buy it. When he appeared on my doorstep with the manuscript under his arm, I at first thought that he was bringing me proofs. But the pages were completely devoid of notes.

"I cannot publish this," he said. "People would not believe it. They would consider it an insult to common decency. I am shocked that you would write such a thing."

But he misunderstood my intention!

I gathered that the time was not yet ripe to expose my friend's vulnerability and pain to the world. People wanted to hear about his victories, not his defeats. It was just as Inspector Ledvina had said to me in Prague. It was the illusion that sold his stories. And this manuscript had stripped it away.

In the end Mr Doyle and I came to a compromise.

Write another of our adventures from happier times when Holmes was a flawless and unstoppable force in the fight against evil.

I thus returned *Golem's Shadow* to its chest and to my memories. Sherlock Holmes did not permit me to destroy it. Perhaps the time for its publication will come.

John
H. Watson, M.D.
October 31,
1924

Also from MX Publishing

MX Publishing is the world's largest specialist Sherlock Holmes publisher, with over a hundred titles and fifty authors creating the latest in Sherlock Holmes fiction and non-fiction.

From traditional short stories and novels to travel guides and quiz books, MX Publishing cater for all Holmes fans.

The collection includes leading titles such as *Benedict Cumberbatch In Transition* and *The Norwood Author* which won the 2011 Howlett Award (Sherlock Holmes Book of the Year).

MX Publishing also has one of the largest communities of Holmes fans on Facebook with regular contributions from dozens of authors.

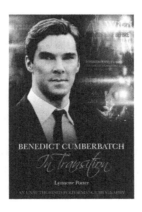

www.mxpublishing.com

Also from MX Publishing

Sherlock Holmes Short Story Collections

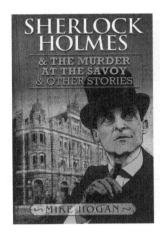 

Sherlock Holmes and the Murder at the Savoy

Sherlock Holmes and the Skull of Kohada Koheiji

Look out for the new novel from Mike Hogan
– *The Scottish Question.*

www.mxpublishing.com

Also from MX Publishing

  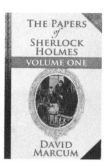

Our bestselling books are our short story collections;

'Lost Stories of Sherlock Holmes', 'The Outstanding Mysteries of Sherlock Holmes', The Papers of Sherlock Holmes Volume 1 and 2, 'Untold Adventures of Sherlock Holmes' (and the sequel 'Studies in Legacy) and 'Sherlock Holmes in Pursuit', 'The Cotswold Werewolf and Other Stories of Sherlock Holmes' – and many more......

www.mxpublishing.com

Links

MX Publishing are proud to support the Save Undershaw campaign – the campaign to save and restore Sir Arthur Conan Doyle's former home. Undershaw is where he brought Sherlock Holmes back to life, and should be preserved for future generations of Holmes fans.

Save Undershaw   www.saveundershaw.com

Sherlockology   www.sherlockology.com

MX Publishing   www.mxpublishing.com

You can read more about Sir Arthur Conan Doyle and Undershaw in Alistair Duncan's book (share of royalties to the Undershaw Preservation Trust) – *An Entirely New Country* and in the amazing compilation Sherlock's Home – The Empty House (all royalties to the Trust).

Lightning Source UK Ltd.
Milton Keynes UK
UKOW06f1804190615

253833UK00005B/240/P